M000074331

THE BEST THING THAT CAN HAPPEN TO A MAN IS TO GET LOST

Alain Gillot

THE BEST THING THAT CAN HAPPEN TO A MAN IS TO GET LOST

*Translated from the French
by Katherine Gregor*

Europa
editions

Europa Editions
8 Blackstock Mews
London N4 2BT
www.europaeditions.co.uk

This book is a work of fiction. Any references to historical events,
real people, or real locales are used fictitiously.

Copyright © Flammarion, Paris, 2017
First Publication 2022 by Europa Editions

Translation by Katherine Gregor
Original title: *La meilleure chose qui puisse arriver à un homme, c'est de se perdre*
Translation copyright © 2022 by Europa Editions

All rights reserved, including the right of reproduction
in whole or in part in any form

A catalogue record for this title is available from the British Library
ISBN 978-1-78770-431-2

Gillot, Alain
The Best Thing That Can Happen to a Man Is to Get Lost

Art direction by Emanuele Ragnisco
instagram.com/emanueleragnisco

Cover design and illustration by Ginevra Rapisardi

Prepress by Grafica Punto Print – Rome

Printed and bound in Great Britain by Clays Ltd, Elcograf S.p.A.

CONTENTS

To Herbie and Duda, who were playing Gershwin that night
at the Walt Disney Concert Hall in Los Angeles.
For their dedication and their smiles.

To Louise and Ulysse, our children.

"But man is not made for defeat.
A man can be destroyed but not defeated."
—Ernest Hemingway

THE BEST THING
THAT CAN HAPPEN TO
A MAN IS TO GET LOST

PART ONE
THE DEAF MAN'S SON

I'd gotten all my things ready and was now in the kitchen, drinking coffee on my feet. It was just after 4 A.M. At this time, it would be no problem to drive across Paris and get to the highway. By dawn I'd already be a long way away, and, all going well, by sunset I'd have reached the South.

Cécile was asleep, and I had no intention of waking her up. Last night, we'd had a disagreement about this trip. We were in the bathroom. She began by saying she found it peculiar that I should choose to drive all that way when Nice is just an hour by plane. Then she wondered, and not for the first time, about the "mercenary" job, as she calls it, I've turned into my area of expertise. At one point she looked at me in the mirror as I stood behind her, leaning against the wall. She'd removed her make-up from one eye but not the other. A cotton ball in her hand. She wasn't hostile and searched for the right words not to offend me. I felt she was hesitating to formulate her question, so I helped her. "You think I lack ambition?"

"Yes," she replied, wiping the other eyelid with the cotton ball.

That's exactly what a director, disconcerted by my behavior, had told my agent a few years earlier. I'd written a version of his movie, which he'd practically dictated to me, then he'd listed me in the credits as consultant and thanked me alongside the service providers. Still, he must have been reasonably pleased with my work, since he offered me another collaboration, but, much to his surprise, I immediately turned it down.

Did it have something to do with my status as an author? Not at all. Was I unhappy with my fee? Not that either. Of course, I could have taken him to court, since, technically, I was the film's co-author, and especially since it had been a box office success, but it had been his idea, his words, and even if his take on rights was rather cavalier, I didn't feel cheated in any way. On the contrary, I thought I had been handsomely remunerated for being his secretary. No, the true reason for my refusal lay elsewhere. His company bored me, and I found it hard to concentrate when he gave me instructions, while his colleagues would quake in their boots when he as much as raised an eyebrow. It was clear that with the kind of willpower that drove him, he would build an empire, something which, as a matter of fact, eventually came to pass, but working for him meant giving up my freedom. And that was too high a price to pay.

I closed the apartment door as softly as I could and went down the stairs to the parking lot. As I rushed down the steps, I couldn't suppress an exquisite sense of escape.

The exchange Cécile and I were having about ambition had carried on in the bedroom. Turning over on her side, she said she'd had a stressful day, then she suddenly remembered something very important. She slipped a DVD into my baggage I absolutely had to watch, the work of a budding genius she wanted to introduce me to when I got back. "It's a unique opportunity, Antoine. Everyone agrees he'll go very far . . ."

There was a somewhat solemn look in her eye, and I realized this was the final chance for me to get my act together. We were lying in bed, side by side. The walls, the painting, the furniture all seemed like a set, with us inside it as though striking a pose. I felt like laughing but stopped myself.

As I walked across the silent parking lot, I remembered Cécile's face in the mirror and her worried way of assessing me. I didn't exactly put her mind at rest—that much I know.

How long have we been living together? Two years? More

like three. We met at the premiere of a blockbuster from across the Pond. Cécile is a journalist for a movie monthly, and that night she needed to get in touch with Jonathan Bowe, one of the actors in the film. We chitchatted at the buffet until she realized I'd had a part in writing the screenplay and tweaked a few scenes shot in Paris, and from then on all her questions focused on Bowe. As it happened, I had become friendly with him. Like me, he played tennis, and when we'd met again before the screening, he'd invited me to join him at a restaurant where he was going to have dinner with the studio big shots. I had no intention of attending this socialite event, but no sooner did Cécile hear that than she grabbed my arm and wouldn't let go, so not only did we join Bowe, but she even obtained her interview. A week later, she called to invite me to her favorite Japanese restaurant, by way of thank you, and we had a brilliant evening. Shortly after that, we started dating.

What brought us together is quite simple. Neither of us is interested in passion and even less in starting a family. We hate conflict and are both jealous of our independence. It's a bit like being business partners. Cécile is attractive, sociable, and funny, especially when tipsy. We don't have an unbridled sex life, and that's not a problem either. Each can pleasure the other, given that he or she shows desire. Our jobs are complementary, and we can help each other out. The one thing that separates us is, indeed, ambition. I don't give Cécile what she has every right to expect, I can see that quite clearly. She wants to climb the social ladder, and I'm not doing everything necessary to help her up. One could almost say that I go out of my way not to succeed. This trip is yet another example. Why does this assignment appeal to me? It's not for the professional goal it represents, of that Cécile is fully aware. What appeals to me is to hit the road, stop off wherever I like, watch the countryside scroll by, and let my mind roam. Then, once I'm on the set, it's to do this work-for-hire as best I can so it takes up neither too much time nor energy, so that I may treat myself to a game of tennis as a reward. How can I explain the fact that I'm so distant from everything? I've given up on it, but I admit it must be disconcerting.

I unlocked the door and slipped behind the wheel of the Jaguar. It's an F-Type coupe, an excellent long-distance vehicle, a present to myself for my fortieth birthday. That time, I drove all night, alone, just so I could listen to the music of the six cylinders, watch the dashboard at work, turn corners at high speed, and assess the excellence of the chassis. Seeing my blissful face after I returned from my nocturnal escapade, Cécile pointed out that I really had to consider growing up. No doubt she was right, now more than ever.

There's something incorrigible about me. The years go by, but I'm still the little boy who used to take roundabout ways to school and walk through the gates only at the last possible minute, as the bell was ringing. One whose sole concern during class was to avoid being called on, avoid being noticed by the teacher to the point of becoming invisible, constantly looking out into the schoolyard, waiting for recess. Nothing's changed, actually. Especially not after everything life has shown me. I still can't bring myself to take human enterprise seriously and only get involved in it as long as it's not too inconvenient. To be totally honest, I can't find a single role I consider essential to hold on to, and nothing has any real importance for me except this precious recess I do my best to create whenever I can.

The highway was almost deserted, and I put the radio on, recognized the crisp touch of Herbie Hancock playing Gershwin on the piano. This is how one should live, managing to balance relaxation and precision.

The movie I have to work on has a substantial budget, but, after a series of problems that occurred during the shoot, there are significant cuts to be made in the screenplay. The producer,

Aurélien Belmer, a man you can't avoid in the industry and whose company is backed by a powerful multimedia group, was waiting for me on location to give me instructions. We'd spoken on the phone, and although he sounded very pleasant, his nervousness was palpable. I already knew that my first task wasn't going to be to alter scenes but to reassure him. That's often the case.

I'm a movie consultant, a script doctor, as they say, or a ghost writer, if you prefer. I write under dictation and never sign my work, which is rather handsomely paid. How did I come to practice this profession? It would be dishonest of me to put it down to chance. After all, I've always written on behalf of others. When I was in the army, I was paid in ciga-rettes to compose love letters and requests to the management. And when it came to finding a job, a companion from the bar-racks, who remembered this little talent of mine, got me into a magazine devoted to sports cars, where my duties consisted in "brushing up" texts in exchange for race-driving lessons. And that's where I got my taste for cars. Then, a few years later, I met the host of a documentary series devoted to the wonders of nature across the world. I became something of his double, traveling with him, writing his commentaries, preparing his studio appearances, until the day when, on the tennis court, he introduced me to a movie producer who was desperately look-ing for someone to doctor his screenplay.

I soon got a hunch that this activity was right up my street. You just need to be tuned in and quick on your toes. As long as you have a modicum of a system, you can have a lot of free time, and, most importantly, the benefit of huge flexibility. Which is my number one priority. So what if a producer behaves abominably? No point getting mad. After all, I only have to put up with him for a few days. What if I don't like the director? I decline his offer under the pretext that my timetable is chockablock. My work is criticized? I already have another job begging for me. Moreover, I noticed that in a movie project, the author always ends up getting in the way because he's the father of the plot and, sooner or later, must be killed off, whereas the consultant is called out and longed for like a plumber on a Sunday night when the kitchen is flooded. And the best thing about it is that he is given respect whether he has talent or not, because by the time the quality of his contribution gets truly assessed, he's long gone.

2

I stopped off after Lyons. It had been light for ages. I filled up with gas and bought a sandwich, then I stopped in a parking lot to read *L'Équipe*. A guilty pleasure I indulge in. I can peruse every page in minute detail, dissect the most trivial results. Nothing is alien to me, there's nothing that I'm indifferent to. An article about hockey commandeers my attention as much as an analysis of the most recent matches of the Champions League, or the account of a triathlon in Hong Kong. I don't just read the text. I consider the rankings, the time, and the score. Don't ask me why, because there's nothing rational about it.

My phone vibrated. It was an SMS from Paul, my agent. "Can I call you in ten minutes?"

There's something mysterious about our relationship, for him as well as for me. He's from an upper middle class family, mind-blowingly well educated, looks down on sports, and believes only in the virtue of work. You could say he's my direct opposite.

His agency, deliberately small, represents just a handful of well-known actors and writers who have perfected the art of being demanding. So how did he end up looking after me? It all came about in peculiar circumstances, at his mother's funeral. I wasn't invited but, that day, had to pick up a precious document from the hands of a production manager who was supposed to attend the ceremony, and who couldn't come up with a better option than giving me an appointment at the main entrance of the Père Lachaise cemetery. Except that he didn't show up at the agreed time, so, after waiting for a while in the heavy rain, I decided to go into the cemetery. I roamed down the paths until I noticed a gathering. I'd begun looking for the man who'd stood me up when there was a sudden stir and shouts of indignation in the crowd. Two men were fighting, and people were trying to pull them apart. One of them had a bloody nose; the other's shirt was torn. But that wasn't the worst. As I drew closer, I saw that the coffin was stuck at an angle in the grave, halfway down. It must have slipped out of the undertakers' hands, and they couldn't pull it back up in spite of all their efforts. Were these two events connected? It was impossible to tell but, in any case, everybody's attention was focused on the fight, so much so that the funeral had become a low priority. That's when I noticed a man of about forty with a rose buttonhole standing apart from the commotion, sheltering in one of the vaults. His emaciated face was so frighteningly pale, he looked about to faint. I walked up to him, and just as I was about to speak to him, he staggered, forcing me to grab him by the arm, which was no thicker than that of a child. Later, Paul told me I was gripping him so tightly in the path that he felt compelled to follow me.

So this is how we ended up together on Boulevard de Ménilmontant, in a brasserie devoted to gambling with a floor littered with cigarette butts. It took me a while to realize that he was the son of the deceased, Françoise Marquais, "the great Françoise," as her friends—and her enemies, actually—called her. At the time, he had already taken over control of the agency. His mother, vanquished by throat cancer, had obviously resigned herself to entrusting him with the keys to the kingdom, but, apparently, nobody had noticed the handover of power yet. We ordered a bad rum, and, after a moment of silence, Paul had begun speaking in that very distinct, I'd say aristocratic, voice of his, and remarked on the fact that his mother's funeral fit the relentless pattern perfectly. He said that all her life she'd been surrounded by people who didn't care two hoots about her son, who didn't even know she had one, and that she'd never done the slightest thing to set the record straight. He'd always had to fight, even just to get to her office and see her between meetings. As for obtaining a look or a kiss from her, that was out of the question. And now, at the cemetery, he'd felt the same as at the agency. All this high society had settled their business without even knowing he existed, and that was the natural order of things.

At this point, Paul had downed the contents of his glass, then wondered out loud, "Even so, a coffin that gets stuck at an angle in the grave, that never happens, right?"

I then remembered my own mother's death and told him about how, after the doctor had come to issue the death certificate, the undertaker's technicians had gotten hold of the body to empty it of its contents with some kind of vacuum, but for some reason the machine had gone wrong, generated air instead of sucking it out, and turned her hapless belly into a soccer ball about to explode. I obtained the desired effect. Paul burst into giggles, then wondered how he could possibly not be aware of my name, since he was reading the industry yearbook before bed by the time he was ten.

Death either separates men or brings them together. In our case, it had forged an indestructible alliance, even better than a contract. One thing led to another, and Paul, a man who only loved integrity, who worshipped authors, ended up looking after me, a ghostwriter, an opportunistic scribe.

"Am I disturbing you?" Paul asked.

"No. I'm in a highway service area."

"What are you doing?"

"I'm reading the paper and eating a ham and cheese sandwich."

"Have you read the screenplay?"

"Yes."

"And?"

"It's the *Odyssey* transposed into a thriller on the Riviera."

"Really?"

"A real estate mogul whose name could be Ulysses miraculously escapes a murder attempt. He realizes that the man who ordered the killing is a Russian mafia guy who not only is his business rival but also covets his wife and, in order to obtain her favors, traps his son in some nasty business. However, the hero's wife resists while the hero has his face redesigned and gets himself hired, incognito, as a servant in his own house."

"It's the return of Ulysses to Ithaca."

"There you go."

"And what's the writing like?"

"It's okay."

"I really must talk to you about another project," Paul said, moving on. "It's the remake of a cult movie. I'm certain you'll have fun with it, and it's outrageously well paid."

"You can do that when I get back. I'm away for forty-eight hours, perhaps even less."

"I sometimes wonder how you do it."

"I avoid thinking."

"I don't believe you."

"You should."

"Let's speak tomorrow, then."

"Alright."

I went back to my reading. The rugby page was devoted to the Wallabies' European tour. In a very well-constructed boxed text, their coach highlighted the importance of a pass after contact in modern playing. It started to drizzle, but I kept the car door open and my feet swinging out. I'd told Paul the truth. I always do. It's true that I avoid thinking when I write. I get told a story, and I rewrite it. Any pieces of the jigsaw missing? Then I suggest several solutions and keep the one my employers prefer, and if, at the next stage, they do a U-turn, which happens regularly, then I buckle down with this new premise without making a fuss. The important thing is that the client's happy. Writing is my work tool. It must meet just one criterion, and that's to allow me a pleasant life. This may sound shocking. I realize that. Many people consider writing holy. It's a kind of initiation quest, reserved for the select few. I'm not one of them, sorry. Every now and then a colleague will ask me, slightly irritated, where I get this "utilitarian" approach to my job. I reply that it's because I'm the deaf man's son, and immediately change the subject.

I don't like talking about myself. I'm not an intellectual. I prefer to play a down-the-line backhand, because that's when I really feel I'm expressing myself. As for my father, I think I'm right in saying this, his infirmity influenced my relationship with writing. He was completely deaf in one ear and almost entirely so in the other. He wore a hearing aid that distorted sounds horribly and would always end up cursing the whole world and tearing it off, taking refuge in his silence. We had a difficult relationship. He thought I talked behind his back and mumbled when facing him so that he wouldn't understand anything. He would fly into terrible rages until the day it occurred to me to write him little notes, either for everyday things or in order to clear up misunderstandings, and this method seemed to suit him. Things would get tense again between us, but for the procedure to be successful I had to reply on the spot, clearly and concisely, and that's how I gradually became skilful at this exercise.

No strangers came to this suburban house my grandmother had bought for her daughter after the war, across the street from the municipal undertaker. She herself lived on the second floor, in two rooms set aside for her, a bedroom and a kitchen, which you could access through a narrow door called the communicating door—now you couldn't make up something like that.

We lived isolated, my grandmother, my mother, my father, my two sisters, and I. No friends, no cousins, a TV set at the end of the table with a wire connected to my father's ear, my mother who ate in the kitchen after she'd served our soup, and me, who couldn't wait to go back to my room where I would devise plans of escape.

It's no doubt because of this confinement that I was painfully shy. I didn't have a single friend and felt totally unable to come on to a girl, even though I was desperately in love with the one I sat next to in French class. All I managed to do was follow her from a distance when she went back home, not far from where I lived. It was daily torture not having the courage to speak to her. Once I was back home, I'd take refuge in my room and stay there, mulling over my misfortune while looking out the window at the undertaker's workshop where they built coffins. I could see the staff hide bottles of wine in the boxes, reduce bodies when they got the measurements wrong, stuff parsley up the nostrils of the corpses, and it was from watching this implacable final reality that my determination was born: I didn't want to die without having lived.

That's when I got the idea of using the procedure that had worked so well with my father. I wrote a few words on a piece of paper, folded it carefully, and, the following day, my heart pounding, gave it to the young lady as she was leaving school. The result was beyond my expectations. She smiled, started talking to me very naturally, as though she had just been waiting for this gesture from me, and as we walked down that sidewalk, my elbow brushing against hers, I felt incredibly happy and strong. I had overcome my fear. Thanks to a few words. If this was all it took, then I could always find words and put them together as required, whenever life became a bit of a struggle.

There was a rumble of thunder. Large drops started hammering on the windscreen. Time to get back on the road. I suddenly realized that death has always been very present in my life. I was born across the road from an undertaker, I met my agent in a cemetery, and my most important piece of work so far has been to adapt Céline's novel *Death on the Installment Plan*, even though the screenplay is still in a drawer. The first girl I ever kissed, when I was sixteen, said I was obsessed with death. Is there a connection between my love of playing hooky and my hours spent watching coffins being built? It's not impossible.

As soon as I left the access road, I noticed the traffic becoming heavier, just enough to make driving interesting. I love sliding into the stream of cars, anticipating the reaction of other drivers while stopping myself from using the brake. That's my one little talent, after all, bypassing obstacles, but I've turned it to good account. I managed to escape from the family tomb, turned my solitude into a pleasant job, my girlfriend is lovely even if we don't always see eye to eye, and my spin serve wreaks havoc on the court. I'm bloody lucky, actually. In three hours at most, I'll have reached my destination.

3

T he map sent to me by the production company was clear. At Cap-Martin, take the D 43 as far as the village of Martouret, then turn right into a slightly narrower road that goes into a pine forest. It was impossible to miss the villa, since it stood on a hill overlooking the bay. I wondered how this kind of land could have been declared fit for construction. The owner must have had friends in the right places.

I drove at least three hundred meters alongside a high wall, which gave me an idea of the size of the area, and soon saw barriers rise before me, as well as technical trucks from which a trainee emerged to guide me to the parking lot. "I'll take you to the production manager," he said. "It's a bit of a walk."

He can't have been older than seventeen, so it must have been his first shoot. His equipment smelled new, and he'd bought the kind of knife you need to survive in the Amazon but which just ends up opening beer bottles.

"You've arrived at a slightly odd time," he added. "There's been a clash between the director and the leading actress. It all started with a swimsuit she said was too revealing. So now we're waiting for another one, made to measure, which should be delivered by plane, and everything is at a standstill."

You could make out the futuristic lines of the villa through the vegetation. The trainee stopped at a distance and used his walkie-talkie to request permission to approach. He already knew the answer but was still at the stage of being overzealous.

They'd laid down some tracks around the swimming pool

for a dolly, and two cameras equipped with different lenses were waiting patiently on their wagons. A spaghetti-esque mess of cables was snaking on the ground, the lighting was in place, as was the video playback. Even the actors' chairs had been set up, except that they were vacant and the technical team had deserted the set. There was only an assistant director there to watch over the equipment who, overcome by the heat, had nodded off at the foot of the crane.

We walked around the villa and arrived at the production manager's office. He had set himself up at the back, on a terrace shielded by a porch roof. He was in the middle of a phone call that sounded difficult and was scribbling over his schedule as he went along. Since the conversation continued for a while, I glanced at the timetable and saw that Scene 32 was the order of the day. Whenever I discover a screenplay, I try to summarize every scene so I can memorize its structure, which saves precious time all round.

I remembered that Scene 32 corresponded to a key moment of the plot. The hero's wife is sunbathing on the terrace, and the Russian mafia guy comes to harass her in her privacy, right in front of the gardener, who is none other than the allegedly dead husband, returned among his nearest and dearest to seek revenge. At one stage, the gangster gets pushy, and the hero is tempted to intervene, thereby putting his secret plan in danger. I wondered if, in the credits, they would mention that it had been "freely adapted from Homer" or thank the latter alongside the service providers.

Once he'd finished his phone call, the production manager noticed our presence, and, once again, I stated who I was and my reason for coming to the shoot.

"I'll let Monsieur Belmer know you're here. Would you like a coffee?"

"Yes, please."

"The machine is just there, at the corner. I'll be right back."

I got myself an espresso and took a stroll on the terrace that looked down on the grounds. Away from the villa, on a lawn manicured like a golf course, a majestic tent had been erected, with rugs outside the entrance, like something out of *Lawrence of Arabia*.

"See that?" the production manager said, coming back to me. "Goran brought it back from a commercial shoot in the Emirates. We had to connect water and electricity and, since he eats all his meals there, hire staff for him . . ."

The director he was talking about, Goran Tosik, had built a solid reputation with steamy thrillers for Hollywood, but had gotten involved in a drugs case and hastily moved to Europe in order to escape the US authorities. The latest commercial he'd shot for Mercedes had definitely established his scandalous reputation as a director. He'd used girls in leather bodysuits and garter belts rubbing themselves against the radiator grill of a new model of sports station wagon, supposed to represent the height of refinement and advanced technology.

The production manager leaned over the guardrail. He had broad shoulders, but one could sense that he was beginning to buckle under the weight of his responsibility.

"How did you get here?"

"I drove."

"Put all your expense accounts in an envelope for me, alright? And don't come asking me for money six months down the line and without any receipts, like all the tin-pot stars. You're staying in Cap-Martin. Belmer will come pick you up in a helicopter. He's staying on a boat moored in the bay."

"Sounds like a luxurious shoot."

"Don't remind me. Also, give me your car keys and leave your baggage inside. We'll make sure everything gets to the hotel."

"Thank you."

"Oh, God, I don't know if there's anything you can do, but

please get things moving. We're already ten days behind schedule. Believe me, I've seen some bloody messes in my time, but
this, really . . ."

"The trainee told me something about a swimsuit."

"Today it's the swimsuit, tomorrow it'll be the color of the
water. I don't give a shit about their fucking turf war. I just
want one of them to kill the other so this fucking ship keeps
sailing!"

A man came out of the tent, and I recognized the skull,
smooth as an egg, of Goran Tosik. I remembered an interview
he gave *Rolling Stone*, in which he declared his unconditional
love for Godard because, he claimed, he'd "fucked" everybody.

"Do you know what he does when he's not filming?" the
production manager continued. "He goes shooting. He's pals
with a Secret Service guy who sticks to him like glue. They
have a whole arsenal in their trunk, and they go into the pine
forest and improvise a rifle range. This job will be the death of
me. Ah, your taxi's here . . ."

He indicated with his chin a fast-approaching dot of light in
the sky. It looked like a UFO, but it was just the sun glowing
on the helicopter cabin. Down below, Goran was talking with
the security men and playing at being a trainer with their dog.
He'd put his arm in its mouth and was roaring with laughter,
but when the noise of the rotor reached his ears, he went back
into his tent. We were slap-bang in the middle of mythology.

The trainee came to pick me up on a quad bike, and I
climbed on behind him. We drove as far as the clearing where
the helicopter had landed. The pilot kept the blades spinning,
and I went beneath them and hauled myself up into the cabin,
where Belmer was waiting for me. He was wearing a double-
breasted jacket with a coat of arms, flannel pants, and moc-
casins from Vieto. He looked like Cary Grant. He kissed my
cheeks as though we'd known each other for ages—people are

quick to kiss in this industry, and as quick to strangle one another at the first disagreement.

"See what a mess?" he exclaimed. "At this rate, we might as well be dumping sacks of banknotes on the beach!"

The pilot pushed down the lever, and we flew up into the air, with Belmer shouting in my ear in order to be heard above the surrounding racket.

"Tosik could have perfectly well shot other scenes today, but he found every possible excuse not to alter the schedule. And you know why? He wants the budget to rocket so I'm forced to bring other financial partners into the movie and give jobs to his pals, like Sony Pictures or those smart asses New Line. All this just so he can get his hands on the final cut, but I'm not going to put up with that. You're my trump card!"

The Colibri flew in a large circle, and through the porthole I saw villas with so much direct access to the sea that public beaches were reduced to almost nothing. Evidently, over here the management of the coast was viewed from a very personal perspective. At this moment, we were flying over the liquid element. The sun was low, and the wavelets were sparkling. The pilot indicated a spot on the water, someone swimming in the blue waters of the bay. He drew nearer. It was a young woman. She swam in a lithe, rhythmical way and exuded a surprising sense of ease, I'd say even freedom, perhaps because she was far away from the shore. I couldn't take my eyes off her and kept track of her until she was out of our field of vision. The pilot stepped on the gas in order to fly straight towards the open sea, and Belmer grabbed my arm to bring me back to reality—his, at least.

"I've ordered for nobody to disturb us. It'll take us a couple of hours to nail the problem. Dorfman speaks very highly of you. He says you saved his picture."

"That's an exaggeration," I replied, trying to play it down.

It's counterproductive to show off in this industry.

Everybody knows everybody, and you end up finding everything out. Dorfman had wanted to show he was "modern" by breaking up the time sequence of his movie. He had literally taken narrative blocks and put them together randomly. The result turned out to be unpalatable, simply because there was no justification for this form. You're not an Iñárritu just because you want to be. All I'd had to do was tell the story in chronological order. It was like a tennis match when the opponent hands you victory on a plate.

The helicopter arrived within sight of a yacht at least forty meters long, equipped with a landing platform. Belmer squeezed my arm a little too hard, and I gathered this was his flagship.

"I hired it for the shoot," he trumpeted. "It's a profitable investment, you know, and a tax-deductible expense. I entertain journalists and movie partners here. By the way, I'm throwing a little party for the board of directors of the channel the day after tomorrow. You think I'll be able to give them the new version of the screenplay?"

"In principle, yes."

"Obviously, I'll need to approve it first."

"It'll be in your inbox tomorrow morning."

"I adore you."

"Don't jump the gun . . ."

As the pilot started his approach, a gust of wind blew us off course, and he had to perform his maneuver again, successfully this time.

Belmer rushed into the elevator that connected the three stories of the boat. I followed him. When we emerged on the main deck, we bumped into the captain, wearing a white jacket with epaulettes, and he greeted us regulation style. It was like *Love Boat*.

We settled down in the saloon that took up the whole back of the ship. Beyond the stern, you could see Menton and the

Italian border. Belmer called his assistant and asked her to join us, and a blonde young woman in a sober suit arrived almost immediately. She placed a script and a USB stick before me, then vanished as quickly as she had arrived. I wasn't able to catch her eye, but I could have sworn she'd been crying.

"You'll see, I've highlighted the scenes I think are weak or superfluous," Belmer said. "I've also annotated those about which I have my doubts."

His phone vibrated.

"It's my legal department. I really must—"

"Go ahead."

He walked away to answer the call, and I started leafing through the screenplay. His directives were in red and his doubts few. In a case like this, it's in the producer's interest to use the consultant's name instead of his brain in order to support the changes he's already considering. This way, he can always justify difficult decisions, especially to the director, by hiding behind the opinion of a "specialist" who, if need be, can also act as lightning rod. The advantage for the consultant is that he's spoon fed, the drawback, that he can't prove to himself how important he is, which, in my case, isn't an issue. Just before reaching Cap, I'd spotted a tennis club that looked perfect. A few well-kept courts, sheltered from the wind.

"Sorry about that," Belmer said, coming back into the saloon. "It's a complex business. We carelessly started work on the adaptation of a novel without acquiring the rights beforehand, and now the author is raising the bidding. Have you had a look at the screenplay?"

"Yes. It all seems very clear. You refocus the movie on the leading actors. A bit less action and more psychological tension."

"It's a tragedy, after all! And in tragedies, what's principally at stake is—"

His phone vibrated again. This time he didn't apologize,

and I wondered what a meeting with him was like when he agreed to be "disturbed." He went back out on the deck. I could see him walking up and down and should have carried on reading, but I decided I'd have all the time I needed to do so at leisure while making corrections directly on the document. Besides, I'd mostly have to delete scenes with a simple click.

I thought again about the young woman we'd flown over in the helicopter. She was very far from the shore. At the time, I had only noticed the ease with which she swam, but what if it was something else, like suicide, for instance? I forced myself to rule out this theory. I was on this yacht to do this job, and I had to remained focused, especially since Belmer had reappeared.

"Where were we?" he asked.

"At tragedy."

"Yes. All the audience wants to see is how the hero avenges himself and eventually gets his wife back. The rest, well . . . I've carried out a simulation. With all these cuts, we're close to saving a million. In any case, feel free to do what you want. Only bear in mind that the closer you are to that threshold, the better. Would you like a drink?"

"No, thanks."

He wasn't just Cary Grant. He was a tactician, and the cuts in the screenplay didn't just reduce the budget but also sent Tosik a message, to remind him who was in charge. He suddenly came close to me.

"And now we must talk about the more delicate aspect of your contribution. I didn't want to mention it on the phone . . ."

His gaze became heavier. He was trying to assess just how far he could trust me. What was this about? Paul hadn't told me, so he clearly he didn't know either.

"Come with me," he said.

He took me down the corridors, to the belly of the ship. We reached a door guarded by a watchman. He explained that it was where the rushes were edited during the shoot.

An editor and his assistant were at work, their eyes fixed on their computer screens; judging by their gray faces, they were chained to this damned movie and had lost count of their sleepless nights. I was often invited to viewings. Sometimes so I could alter a scene at a moment's notice, sometimes to delete one and then assess the consequences in terms of narrative consistency.

"Show us the terrace scene, please," Belmer said.

The chief editor tapped on his keyboard and brought up on his screen a shot in which Carole Aubert, the leading actress, was facing the gangster in a close-up. At first, I didn't notice anything in particular, except that I thought she was overacting a little, but then she said the word "associate." As a matter of fact, all the words with an "s" seemed to cause her an insoluble problem. It wasn't simply a question of pronunciation, because in that case, it would surely have been possible to sculpt the sound—nowadays, technology can produce miracles, the way it can with images. Pronouncing "s" was painful for Carole, so much so that her mouth would clearly twist as she was about to tackle that letter.

"Do you see the issue?" Belmer asked.

"Clearly."

We left the room, and he pulled me aside. His tone of voice had turned confidential. "You know what actors are like. They focus on a detail until they get obsessed. For some time, Carole had felt that her jaw was too prominent. No talking her out of it. She decided to have a reduction. The surgery went perfectly well. It was a careful job, no leak in the magazines, except that, ever since, she's been suffering terrible toothaches, especially when she pronounces certain words. Do you think there's anything you can do?"

"It doesn't seem impossible."

He saw that I meant it. He gave a sigh of relief. Being a producer isn't an easy job.

"The shuttle will drop you off at your hotel. Carole knows you're here, but she thinks your input is limited to budget cuts. So if you happen to bump into her . . ."

"That's not very likely, but if it does, don't worry, I'll be as silent as the grave."

We got into the elevator, and while the voice of Enrique Iglesias escorted us on our way up from the ship's belly, the swimsuit issue caught up with Belmer. I could guess the latest developments by the content of his replies. The manufacturer had accomplished a feat to ensure that the bespoke model was already completed, but it still had to be brought to the shoot, and the poor man was concerned that nobody had shown up. And yet Belmer had chartered a private jet for the occasion, appointed the most high-performance carrier, and couldn't understand the reason for this new delay. I could see him trying to channel his anger. I was worried his assistant would cry again, as would the whole production team, since it was outrageous that he should be the one to have to solve this kind of problem.

As we reached the top deck, he managed to free himself from the phone call. He put his hand on my shoulder, as though he'd made a friend. Did he have even one in the world? Frankly, I wasn't sure.

"I look forward to getting your text."

A crew member came to take me to the pontoon. The motorboat was beside the yacht, so I just jumped in.

In the end, we never did have the two hours of calm he'd promised, but then it was always like that.

4

The sailor checked that I had settled onto my seat, then started the motor gently. It was a bit choppy, and he didn't want to rock me too much.

The sun had set, night was falling, and the coastline was beginning to light up. The image of the swimmer flashed before me. The way she sliced through the water. I turned to the pilot.

"You didn't happen to see a woman swimming in the open sea late this afternoon?"

"Yes, I did. She had quite a nerve. We went over to her. We didn't think it was right for her to be so far out. We even offered to take her back to shore."

"And what happened?"

"She refused point blank. She continued swimming for a while longer, then turned around and returned at the same speed. Do you know her?"

"No, not at all."

"I reckon she swims competitively. You know when swimmers train, they do several kilometers a day."

His comment was pertinent, and I felt relieved. Even so, my curiosity had been aroused, and I wanted to ask him what the young woman looked like but thought better of it. How would it help me to know? So I'd start dreaming about a stranger? That wasn't like me. I've always found it ridiculous when, for years on end, people pursue a figure they walked past on an embankment, endowing a stranger with unique qualities under the pretext that they're sure they'll never find them again. I thought this kind of mental construction was the best way to miss out on your own life.

The hotel had a private pontoon, and the pilot approached it with a skilful maneuver. He didn't need to dock because I was already on land, my bag over my shoulder, gesturing good-bye.

The coolness of the sea rose between the boards of the pontoon. I suddenly felt like slowing down. If there's one power I could have possessed—from a spiritual point of view, naturally—it would have been to stop time or slow down its progress whenever things became more sensitive. I knew how to slalom around obstacles and juggle situations, but there was something else, something finer, a sense of being in the world, that drifted in the shadow of this pontoon, and which escaped me. I could only get a glimpse of it, the same way I could glimpse the light glowing on the water in the gaps between the boards.

I reached the hotel entrance. The porter was on the front steps, smoking, and the way I emerged from the shadows gave him a start. He quickly threw away his cigarette and straightened his cap to open the doors of the kingdom for me. There weren't many people in the lobby at that time of day. The patrons had mostly gone out or were dining in the restaurant. The concierge handed me an electronic key and delivered a message.

"Madame Aubert asked us to let her know when you arrive."

"Please don't. I have a lot of work, and it's rather late. I'll have dinner in my room."

"Very well, monsieur."

I got into the elevator. Carole Aubert was a former beauty queen and had been denied a future in the art of the cinema, yet she had worked like crazy, studied with a disciple of

Strasberg's, had even ventured onto the stage, and, although auteurs still looked down on her, she had a perfectly respectable career in so-called commercial pictures. I wasn't surprised that she wanted to see me. Actors are always jumpy when they hear that the screenplay is going to be altered, and even if the production company swears that their part is in no way affected by these changes, they never quite believe it. Even so, I had nothing to gain by meeting her. More than once, either on the set or while doctoring a screenplay, I had come across the most extraordinary tricks of seduction on the part of leading actors whose aim was to take control of the writing. As far as I was concerned, these relationships based on self-interest were skewed from the start, and when any of my fellow screenwriters fell into the trap and then complained about how superficial the film world was, I quite happily pointed out their naivité—their hypocrisy even, seeing how blatantly obvious the trick was and how predictable its outcome.

The room the production company had booked for me was on the third floor, overlooking the park. The suites with a view of the sea must have been reserved for VIPs, but given what I needed to do there, this one was perfect. I opened the French windows wide to enjoy the night, threw my shoes away from me, and got down to work. Once I'd checked that the file contained on the USB stick corresponded to the annotated screenplay, I began to thin out the text.

Just as I had worked out at first glance, Belmer wasn't suggesting anything extravagant. He had simply deleted all the scenes featuring minor characters, as well as a few stunts. He'd done it in order to cut his budget, but that didn't make it any worse. In three or four places, he'd gone a little far and compromised the overall coherence, but that was easy to prove, and I took the time to draft a note to that effect.

When doctoring a screenplay, to whatever degree, it's important not to neglect a pedagogical approach. The success of the venture depends on it. Each version of the screenplay has its backstory and is generally a collective effort. A script doctor is like a visitor welcomed into a home. He may have an opinion about the decor, immediately see the advantage in knocking down such or such wall, but he must nevertheless make sure of two things before expressing his opinion: first that he has been asked to do it, then that his remark will not be perceived as a value judgement on what's there but as a suggestion his interlocutor is free to accept or dismiss. Trust me, if you take care to apply this rule, you'll avoid a great deal of trouble.

In addition to that, the script was quite hard to read, which is often the case with the final draft, the one used for the shoot. This may sound paradoxical, since it's supposed to be the result of careful development, but, in actual fact, there will have been so many consecutive layers of writing and re-writing that it ends up looking more like a puzzle than the transcription of an individual's living thought.

Room service delivered my dinner, and I took advantage of it to read over my notes again whilst picking at my plate. There were no shocks or dilemmas for me. It was a done job. I allowed myself a glass of wine, my feet on the desk, then selected Belmer's e-mail address. It was one-thirty A.M., and I'd finished my task. I'd left Paris before dawn, avoided the director's gunfire, escaped the producer's mood swings, and taken care not to have to face the actress's anxieties. Everything was going as well as it could.

I saw that there had been a message from Cécile at eight-thirty, and I wasn't surprised I'd missed it—when I was working, I'd forget about my phone. She hoped I'd had a good trip, that all was going well, but her message was really about something else: she wanted to remind me to watch the potential genius's DVD. Clouds gathered over my horizon. I'd thought I'd earned my freedom, but I was still on parole. I settled on the bed and slid the film into my computer. Better not wait, or I'd be less and less inclined to see it.

It was a medium-length film, in black and white, and I got a bad feeling about it as soon as I saw the opening credits. The title of the film, *Excess*, the first frames, which were trying to be terribly original, and even the font, which was so stylized it was illegible, made me fear the worst, and the rest did nothing but confirm the considerable extent of the artistic damage. Erik Arlo, that was the ambitious young man's name, didn't think it was a good idea to tell a story—that would have been too simplistic an intention for a pioneer of his grandeur. Instead, he chose to treat the viewer to an experimental performance based on pubic hairs, Shakespeare quotes, and desolate landscapes. The whole thing was twenty-two minutes, forty-seven seconds long, which felt like an eternity, and yet I forced myself to watch it a second time. It was practically a reflex when I was overwhelmed with hatred, because sometimes extreme opinions spring from a temporary state of mind, or from annoyance at a single detail that, despite your best efforts, spreads to everything. However, my second viewing did nothing but confirm my first, and even toughened my final verdict, as often happens on appeal.

I lay on the bed, eyes wide open, puzzled. How could Cécile have confused talent and pretentiousness to this extent? And, more importantly, how would I manage to express my honest opinion without increasing the tension between us further? I considered two possible solutions. One was to stall for time, the other to lie. I opted for the first one. The screening of this punishment would take place soon, Cécile had told me, and I thought it highly unlikely that this fraud would not be unmasked on that occasion. It would then be infinitely easier to side with other people's opinion rather than stick my neck out on my own and face a Cécile who was already quite annoyed with me.

At this moment, there was nothing to stop me from running a bath, and I felt my body relax in the warm water. Everything had a solution. All you had to do was keep calm and make a decision only after careful thought. Thank heavens that was in my nature. I suddenly remembered that the US Open had started and that now, given the time difference, unless it was raining in New York, they would be playing in Flushing Meadows.

I put on the hotel bathrobe and settled comfortably on my pillows, holding the remote. Luckily, this luxury establishment offered guests a digital package that included the sports channels, and, after a brief navigation, Roger Federer appeared on the screen, warming up. He was playing a long-limbed Chinese man who was becoming known on the circuit, and whose game revolved around his being at the back of the court with amazing regularity. Their opposing styles promised an exciting match.

Roger (which Swiss exoticism pronounced *Rogeur*) was the first to serve. He had a killer gleam in his eye and a relaxed arm. Whenever he found this balance between wanting to kill his opponent and his natural fluidity, he was almost unbeatable. Thirty-three minutes later, he had won the first set, leaving only two games to his opponent, who, even so, fought over every ball as though his life depended on it. My eyelids began to droop, and I closed my eyes for a moment. I could hear the strikes, the soles screeching on the court, and it was like a lullaby. I could guess how the match was going just by listening to this music.

The Chinese player was hitting the ball harder and harder in order to push the Swiss player back, but Roger kept grabbing his opponent by the throat and finding amazing angles. What was it that I loved so much about what was just a game? Was it the possibility of responding to any situation, whoever the adversary, by being resourceful? It must be. I remembered a remark by John McEnroe, one of the greatest dysfunctional characters this sport has ever known, and incidentally a true genius, unlike Erik Arlo. He said that tennis was a one-man sport with two players. That's exactly it, and that's probably why I felt so at home on a court.

Belmer woke me up. Since he couldn't reach me on my cell, he called the room phone. He was very happy with the new version, so much so that he'd called a meeting with Tosik and the production manager, with a view to using it immediately. Contrary to expectations, Goran had approved the cuts, even though they were many and radical, and found the dialogue suggestions aimed at bypassing Carole Aubert's elocution problems very clever. According to Belmer, this sudden evidence of goodwill must conceal something, like the preparation of a counter-offensive on another front, but for the time being he couldn't care less. He'd cut the budget by a million and warded off the curse of the "s"-s.

These successful decisions made the delay caused by Carole Aubert's swimsuit negligible, and the overall financial gain was so sizeable that Belmer had called my agent to thank him for suggesting me and to assure him of a prompt payment. Prompt payment on the part of a producer was the height of gratitude.

On a roll, he invited me to a party for the movie partners, which he'd mentioned the night before, but I pointed out that I had commitments in Paris. Setting foot on the flagship again was out of the question. It was time for recess.

Besides, what time was it? My cell phone was out of charge, so I glanced out of the picture window. It seemed like late morning, since the sun was already high. I had slept incredibly well.

I had breakfast on the balcony and asked the hotel

concierge for the details of the tennis club I'd noticed when I arrived in Cap. I called right away. There was no partner available, at least not for the next few hours, but one of the instructors, who sounded pretty high level, offered to play with me. It was my ideal solution by far, because it was often risky to confront a local celebrity waiting for nothing better than to crush the passing amateur. Besides being mostly excellent players, instructors tend to have a mindset for exchanging balls without investing a disproportionate ego in the game.

I checked my equipment and picked up my car from the parking lot, animated by an almost childish excitement. In the meantime, I had contacted this instructor, and we'd arranged to meet at two o'clock, which would give us the afternoon to play. I plugged in my cell phone to charge it. Paul had left me a message and, again, so had Cécile, but I decided not to listen to them until after the match. Nobody was going to deprive me of this moment.

My partner was waiting for me at the bar, and we got acquainted in the changing rooms. His name was Stéphane Brisson. He was a tall, sprightly guy with tanned skin and a direct expression. He'd almost made it to the French junior team but had been let down in the middle of his rise to fame by compartment syndrome in his arm, a very painful inflammation of the muscle tissue, which reduces the tone considerably. He'd consulted specialists, had two operations without noticeable progress, and finally decided to play with less intensity, which had cut his path to the top level short. Still, he wasn't bitter; he loved tennis with a passion, and when he realized that by adapting his technique he could continue to play, even make a living from it as an instructor, he considered himself lucky.

We played a few balls to warm up, and I saw immediately how good my day partner was. His physical problem had made him perfect the fluidity of his strike and the intelligence of his tactics so that he could avoid ruptures, for which his arm would have to compensate. Moreover, he had a wonderful frame of mind, was happy for the exchange to last, laughing at strikes he hadn't seen coming. I felt as if I'd known him for ages, even though we'd only been playing for a quarter of an hour.

We decided to start the match and agreed on who'd serve first. He stood behind his line, and I shifted slightly outside the field because during the warm-up I'd noticed that he put a top-spin on his ball, giving it a very marked external effect. He could then drive me outside the court and hit the ball on the fly.

He picked his ball carefully, turned it in his hand several times. That was his routine. Every player has one. That's when *she* came onto the court.

I had time to look over the stranger who was walking toward me without undue haste. She can't have been more than twenty. She was wearing jeans, white flats, and a simple T-shirt. She had an extraordinarily fine figure, but it was her extremely graceful bearing that was especially striking. As for her face, there was something Slav about it, with high cheek-bones, a chiseled nose, and an even mouth. What did she want with me? Her expression, neither aggressive nor particularly friendly, revealed nothing about her intentions.

I glanced to the other side of the net, wishing I could explain this intrusion to my partner, except that I couldn't. That's when the young woman came up to me and slapped me with all her strength.

"They told me I'd find you here," she said with a controlled voice. "I'm glad you're having a good time. As for me, I have plenty of it on my hands, now that you've eliminated my part. Goodbye, monsieur."

Having said that, she turned on her heels and walked away with that light step of hers. She was already at the gate of the court and had vanished behind the hedge of the country club before I'd even had a chance to react. I stood frozen for a moment, my mouth open, then went up to the net to at least apologize to Stéphane, who had remained perfectly composed.

"I should tell you that I don't know that person."

"Did she confuse you with someone else?"

"No, it really was me she was after."

Stéphane was friendly enough for me to provide further details, and I briefly summarized the situation, which perhaps didn't justify such a gesture but at least explained it.

"Would you like to postpone the game?" he asked.

"That would be a shame."

He won the first two games, then I made a comeback, and even led 4-2. He obviously couldn't rely on his forehand, but he varied his strike so skillfully that my lead was no more than a delusion, and he quickly regained the advantage. We were truly enjoying playing together, but that's when my game started to fall apart. I didn't gain any more points until the end of the set, and no more in the following three games, which had never happened to me before. Like any other player, I sometimes experienced a slump in the middle of the match, but never before had I known a fall so brutal that nothing could check it. With that elegance of his, Stéphane tried to save my day by reducing the intensity of the exchange, so subtly that a less seasoned player wouldn't have noticed, but the damage was done. "I'd better stop," I said when it was time to swap sides.

"As you wish. It was fun, wasn't it?"

Stéphane gave me his card, and we promised to meet again on the court next time I was in the area. Then we shook hands, and he didn't make the slightest reference to the young woman, even though he knew as well as I did that she alone was responsible for my quitting.

And yet not once had I thought about her while the balls were flying, or even seen her face before me. Things had occurred much more insidiously. I hadn't doubted either myself or my strikes, as happens when a player's concentration is broken. No, it was in the very game that, as it went on, I had lost interest until it felt absurd to be there. And it was this feeling—totally unusual for me—that had made me leave the match.

I went to my car and drove away from the club slowly, so as not to raise dust, then took the seaside road to return to the hotel. I had to pick up my baggage and go back home. I was in an odd state; the interrupted game had left an unpleasant aftertaste, and I could still feel my cheek burning from the slap. I meant to leave the Jaguar outside the hotel, just long enough to go up to my room, and was very much hoping not to bump into Carole. However, as I got there and the parking valet came toward me, I suddenly accelerated, drove around the flower bank and out through the exit. I guess I couldn't just leave things as they were.

The shoot had obviously resumed, and I parked at a safe distance from the barriers. I bumped into the first assistant director and asked him where the production office was. He indicated an annex to the villa, down the hill. A path led straight there, and I went down it. Beyond the pine trees, I could hear Goran giving orders, then total silence fell on the filming.

What was I doing here? I wasn't the type to run after someone, let alone go searching for anyone, and instead waited for things and people to come to me. I was venturing straight into the unknown.

I found myself outside a shed that must normally be used for storage and that the production company had requisitioned. It was a far cry from Aurélien Belmer's flagship. The office was occupied by two production assistants, phones glued to their ears, and a trainee in the process of taking apart a photocopier. It was cluttered with all the paperwork generated by a film shoot and everything relating to supplies, from toilet paper to coffee machine capsules.

One of the girls finished with her caller.

"Yes, can I help you?" she asked.

Her disenchanted expression suggested she'd worked on quite a few feature films, so it was better to be straight with her.

"I'm a screenwriter," I said. "I've made some cuts to the movie, and I'm looking for someone whose part I've chopped. I'd like to apologize."

"Oh, it's you. You're popular this morning. What does she look like?"

"Brunette, very slim."

She placed a large ring binder in front of me. "If it's the person I'm thinking of, then she's in here."

Both of her phones rang at once, and she grabbed one, making the gesture of a sailor going into a storm.

I opened the ring binder in a corner of her office and started to leaf through it. The entire cast of the movie was there, in alphabetical order, with every actor's picture, an administration form, and other personal details. I braced myself for a boring task but found her face almost immediately. She looked even younger in the photo. Her name was Emma Cassenti. She was twenty-one, born in Meudon. She featured in a scene that I had, indeed, deleted. Three shoot days in a nightclub set, where she was supposed to play a waitress, deliver two lines in three shots, and upset a tray over the baddie. I glanced at the rest of the form. She was a graduate of the École de la rue Blanche and acted more on stage than on the screen. She spoke fluent Italian and had done fencing, dancing, and especially swimming. I felt a little shock. Could it be a coincidence? She had been crawl runner-up of the French minors, and finalist in the butterfly stroke. What was certain was that the swimmer in the bay had impressed me with her grace, just as she had done when she'd walked onto the court, before biting my head off.

"Well?" the assistant asked.

It took a moment for me to surface from my speculations. "I've found her, thanks. What did you do about these parts?"

"We paid their expenses for the number of days pro rata."

"Do you know how I can contact her?"

"Isn't there a phone number on the form?"

"She'll hang up on me."

"The minor roles are staying in the old village, at the Pension Valera. It's on the church square."

I wished her luck, and I'm sure she was about to respond with one of those quips that help you survive a film shoot, but her phones rang again and took her away for good.

The streets leading to the church were very narrow, and I abandoned the Jaguar. The guest house seemed deserted. Most of the actors who'd survived my snip were either on set to be available or having fun at the beach. Still, I managed to find an extra taking a nap and woke him up. He knew very well who Emma Cassenti was. The night before, they'd all ended up at the corner café, playing darts and drinking beer. He thought she was already on the train to Paris. He'd bumped into her in the corridor that morning, and she was asking about the bus times to Menton, where the TGV stopped.

If I took the road that followed the coastline, Menton would be less than half an hour away. All I wanted was to see this young woman and apologize to her. Afterwards, my life would resume its normal course. I realized that the outcome of my trip was uncertain. Emma Cassenti could very well have already gone, having abandoned her idea of taking the train. I knew nothing about her life. Let's just say that I was giving myself a chance to find her but that I wouldn't go out of my way either.

I had difficulty reaching the station because there was road work at the entrance to the town. I left the car in the parking lot and crossed the square, searching for her figure. I thought I saw her at the cab stand, but it wasn't her. I went into the concourse. It wasn't crowded at that time of day, and she wasn't at either the newsstand or at the buffet. I was beginning to think that mine was a ridiculous enterprise when I suddenly saw her. She was buying her ticket at a window. She was wearing a jacket and carrying her travel bag, which she had collected from the guest house, but still exuded the lightness she'd had on the court. I kept my distance but could hear her voice. Apparently, she was presenting the railroad company employee with an insoluble problem and, after a while, decided to give up. She turned around and found herself face to face with me, except that, this time, the surprise element was on my side.

"What are you doing here?" she said.

THE BEST THING · 55

"I wanted to apologize."

The fact that I was there meant I had gone to the production office, then the guest house, and either had sufficient tenacity or been lucky enough to find someone who could tell me she intended to take a train from Menton. I could clearly see her reconstructing the sequence of events in her mind.

"Look," she finally said, "I have a serious problem, so I really don't have time to—"

"I'd like to compensate you."

"Excuse me?"

"Compensate you." That just came to me out of the blue. I had no idea what this offer would actually consist of.

"You don't understand," she continued. "It's not a matter of money but of hours, and there's nothing you can do about that."

"Hours?"

"Temporary employment. Fees."

It must have been obvious from my face that it was all Chinese to me.

"I don't have time to explain it to you," she said a little abruptly.

"What *is* the problem?" I insisted.

At that moment, she could have told me to go to hell or just kept on walking without another word. I put all my chips on the table. "You say you have a problem to solve, so what is it?"

Something in her yielded. She couldn't fight all the battles.

"I need to get to Bordeaux as soon as possible, but it's a real pain from here. I thought to take a plane, but they've all left by now."

"Alright, I'll drive you there."

I heard myself make the offer. I was at Menton train station, with this stranger, and I wanted to ask her if she was the swimmer in the bay but felt that now really wasn't the time.

"Are you serious?"

"If we leave right now, we'll be there in the evening, late, but we'll get there."

She looked at me more intently. She didn't know if she could trust me, which was natural.

"I'll take you to Bordeaux," I said. "I'll drop you off wherever you like, and then you'll never hear from me again. That won't give you your hours, as you put it, but it'll be something."

She was hesitating now, which was some kind of progress. It was as if she had a heap of parameters to consider. Her phone rang, and she walked away to answer it. I didn't know who she was talking to, but the person at the other end of the line must have been highly agitated, and she was obviously trying to calm them down. I got the impression she wasn't getting through to them until there was a moment of silence—the other person must have been exhausted—and at that point she took care to speak slowly, like you do when you're trying to reassure somebody.

Had I gotten too carried away by offering to drive her? After all, it wasn't that outlandish. If she accepted, then I'd be in Bordeaux that night and could drive back to Paris immediately or, if I was too tired, check into a hotel and get a few hours' sleep. That still meant I could be back by mid-afternoon and not jeopardize any of my opportunities. The issue Paul had mentioned wouldn't be decided in just twenty-four hours, and as for the movie genius, I wasn't exactly dying to meet him, but, on the contrary, would have been happy to miss him. And how did Cécile fit into all this? We were heading for an argument, but, just like Paul's business, twenty-four hours wouldn't have made a difference.

When Emma returned, her eyes were still glistening from the battle she'd just had to fight. On the court, in the sunlight, I hadn't noticed how tired she looked. She can't have slept much the night before, and probably not just because of the game of darts. The rings under her eyes gave her face extraordinary depth. As though it summarized all that's luminous and painful in life, that's light-hearted as well as cruel. How could she possibly embody all this at just twenty-one? She put her phone into her bag and lifted her chin. "Alright, you can drive me there."

Stupid as it might sound, her response gave me a sense of victory. I was proud that she should trust me. I could have been anybody, a compulsive womanizer or a pervert. We were about to cross the country together, partly at night. She had allowed for that possibility.

She followed me to the car without a word, and I opened the door for her. I looked at the station clock. It was almost five. We couldn't afford to linger.

"Would you like me to explain about the hours?" she said as she sat down.

"Yes, please."

She was holding her bag against her stomach, as though trying to protect herself from me, just in case.

"As an occasional show business worker, you have to declare five hundred and seven employment hours over a period of ten and a half months if you want to qualify for unemployment benefits. Bearing in mind that rehearsals are rarely taken into account and that contracts can be very short-term, it becomes complicated. If you don't reach your quota of hours, you're entitled to nothing, so you become socially invisible."

She felt better after talking. I could tell. She put her bag at her feet.

"How did you find me this afternoon?" I asked.

"Very easily."

That morning, she'd gone to the administration office because of an issue concerning her social security number missing from her file. The production manager was in the process of listing the cuts to the screenplay to his assistant and hadn't even noticed her. That was how she learned brutally that her part had been cut and, incidentally, to whom she owed this hard-nosed decision. She had then borrowed a bicycle from a trainee and gone to the hotel where the stars were staying, because I was bound to be staying there, and the concierge, not suspecting for a second her plans for revenge, had been only too glad to inform her that I'd gone to the Tennis Club.

"I want to ask you something that might sound a little odd . . ." I said.

I'd been saving this question for a while. Emma tensed up. "If it's about the phone call earlier, I'd rather not talk about it."

"No, it's not about that."

"Then what is it?"

"Did you go swimming in the bay yesterday afternoon?"

"Yes."

I couldn't help but smile. Life really was incredible.

"What's the matter?" she asked.

"Nothing."

I could have told her that I was in the helicopter that had flown over her and about the image I'd had of her in the clear water. But I had to behave like a chauffeur, and a chauffeur keeps his comments to a minimum.

We got onto an almost deserted highway, as is often the case in this part of the Estérel region. The traffic would probably be heavier as we approached Marseilles. I stopped at the first gas station—might as well fill up right away—and Emma got out of the car while I was pouring the gasoline. She wore short jeans that exposed her bare ankles. They were incredibly slim and contributed to the overall grace she embodied. It was as though she was walking on a tightrope.

Once I'd paid for my refill, I parked outside the shop. We bumped into each other at the doors. I was going in as she was coming out.

"Would you like a coffee?" I asked.

"No, thank you."

I selected an espresso at the machine and joined her outside. She was smoking a cigarette, sitting at the edge of the sidewalk, legs stretched out, and I sat next to her, on a concrete kilometer marker.

"Aren't you expected somewhere?" she asked.

"Yes, but I'll be in Paris tomorrow. This is just a detour."

I got the impression she'd asked that partly in order to see if I was a decent man, and wasn't going to come on to her during the trip.

"You're not worried about the distance?" she added.

"No, I like driving."

There was a hint of a smile. She was gradually relaxing.

As we were walking back to the car, my phone vibrated. It was Paul. I opened the door for Emma and gestured that I had to take a call.

"I imagine you must be on your way back," he said.

"Not exactly. I'm just making a detour to Bordeaux, but I'll be there tomorrow, don't worry."

"Why are you going there?"

"I'm driving somebody. It's a long story."

"I see."

"No, you don't."

"That's exactly what people say when—"

"She lost her role because of my cuts, and she had transportation problems."

"So you're being a Good Samaritan."

"Absolutely not."

"Then what are you doing?"

"Okay, I'm being a Good Samaritan. I'll call you as soon as I get to Paris."

I sat back down behind the wheel, and as I was reversing out of the parking lot, I caught the eye of a woman and her

husband, eating sandwiches on a bench. It didn't take a psy-
chic to work out what they were thinking. *Another one of these
guys who bangs much younger women.* I knew appearances, as
well as facts, were stacked up against me. I was crossing France
with a stranger I'd pursued after she slapped me. What could
be more romantic? With Paul, it stopped at a joke, but with
Cécile I was bound to get more insistent questions. I just
hoped that it would be possible for me to convince her with
arguments that put my own mind at rest about my intentions
and removed any ambiguity from the situation.

First, there was her age. I've always found forty-somethings
who chase after their youth by dating young women pathetic.
Secondly, pretty as she was, Emma wasn't my type. I liked
blondes, preferably shapely, always had done. I couldn't help
associating them with gentleness, while I associated brunettes
with a certain degree of aggressiveness. These were terrible
clichés that weren't worthy of me, but, in this case, they were
an excellent safety rail. I'd seen too many apparently level-
headed guys who'd ended up in inextricable situations and lost
everything—job, family, home—because of a heated moment.

"I'm going to get some sleep, if you don't mind," she said.

"Not at all."

She kicked off her ballet flats and tucked her legs under her.

I was driving a little too fast. In a Jaguar, it's easy to hit a
hundred and eighty kilometers per hour without meaning to.
My mind began to drift, and I wondered what was awaiting her
when she arrived. The most likely theory was that she was
involved in a passionate affair. Why else would she be in such
a hurry? I also considered a sick family member, but then she
would have mentioned it. It's the kind of thing one easily
shares. I realized that she had already fallen asleep. I could
hear her breathing, not at all regular, as though she was fighting once again in her sleep. What was she fighting against?

There was something singular about brushing against someone's life like this, about driving someone to their destination and not having any more bearing on their existence than that. Emma's head was turned to the side, and I could see her eyelids quivering slightly. She must have been wavering between waking up and continuing to explore limbo. At that moment, I felt a strange urge to protect her, which I immediately repressed since it was precisely the kind of emotion I had to shield myself from. A few hours from now she would be exiting my life anyway, the same way as she had entered the tennis court: by surprise. I would drop her off at a door, with her bag and her mystery. It was better that way.

PART TWO
AN EXTRAORDINARY FAMILY

1

D riving conditions were very good. No rain, no wind, very little traffic. We reached Marseilles in two hours, and I took the Languedocienne highway through Aix-en-Provence. There was road work at Béziers, and the flow was reduced to a single lane. I slowed down considerably, and Emma opened her eyes.

"Where are we?" she asked.

"Three hours from Bordeaux. Do you mind if I stop? I need to make a phone call."

"Not at all."

I pulled into the parking lot of the next service station, and Emma got out of the car.

"Would you like me to get you anything?" she said.

"No, thanks, I'm fine."

It was time to call Cécile so she wouldn't be surprised by my absence when she woke up in the morning. Her cell phone went to voicemail. At that time, she must have been with her female friends in a bar near the Bastille. I left her a message, as concise as possible, to tell her I wouldn't be back till the afternoon of the following day but that everything was okay. I didn't mention Bordeaux or my passenger. I preferred to tell her in person. Then I headed to the shop, where I couldn't find Emma. She wasn't at the vending machine or in the aisles. I assumed she'd gone to freshen up and did the same, but when I came back from the bathroom, there was still no sign of her. Perhaps she was already outside, smoking. I went back out into the parking lot, walked around the building, and began to explore the surroundings.

Night had fallen, and I felt slightly anxious. I knew so little about her. I realized just how unpredictable this trip was but made an effort not to over-dramatize. I wasn't responsible for this young woman. I was merely doing her a favor.

The rest area extended to a hill planted with trees. I walked toward it, as though drawn by it, my back to the lights. I searched for a form in the midst of the semi-darkness.

"I'm here," I suddenly heard.

I couldn't see anyone nearby.

"Here."

I walked a little farther, guided by her voice, and Emma's form appeared before me at the edge of a cluster of trees. She was standing against a trunk, looking at the nocturnal landscape. She offered me a hazelnut. She had a handful of them. "Try this."

At that moment, beneath the moon, she looked like something straight out of Lewis Carroll, and I wondered if there wasn't a door concealed in the knotty trunk.

"They'll be better a month from now," she added.

I bit into the nut doubtfully, but it was delicious. I'd never imagined you could find this kind of flavor right next to a gasoline depot.

"It looks lovely from here, doesn't it?"

"Yes, it does," I agreed.

The landscape opened onto a plain with vineyards laid out like armies on a battlefield. In the distance, you could see the Mediterranean, which, as the crow flies, can't have been more than fifty kilometers away.

"It was my mother who rang earlier," Emma said. "She got a visit from my brother. He's bipolar and addicted to just about every substance under the sun: pills, drugs, alcohol. He's supposed to be admitted into a clinic near Toulouse. It's very reputable. Apparently, they've had great results."

"Then everything's going to be alright."

"My brother's already had several opportunities to get treatment, but, at the last minute, he always pulls back, and that's when he becomes uncontrollable."

"What do you mean?"

"He can be violent toward other people or toward himself."

"And how does your father fit in to all this?"

"He's dead. He was bipolar, too. He hanged himself at home, and it was my mother who took him down. She's scared my brother will do the same, so she calls me."

We stood silent for a moment. There was a light wind, and the leaves of the hazelnut tree were quivering.

So it wasn't a love affair that was calling her urgently to Bordeaux, but a family problem. I sensed that there was something even more dangerous in this situation, though I couldn't say exactly what.

"We should go," I said. "We've still got a long way to travel."

She couldn't crack one of the shells, so threw it away, ready to tackle the next.

"Am I frightening you with my story?"

"It's not a question of fear."

"You don't give a damn, right?"

"No. But it doesn't really concern me."

"You're just giving me a lift, that's all."

"Exactly."

Why take on unnecessary anxiety by getting involved in dramas that aren't your own? Just once, I lived with a woman with a painful past, Sylvie. She seemed so positive and cheerful that I didn't see it coming, but I gradually realized it was merely a front. I would sometimes find her prostrate, unable to utter a word, after having entertained her friends all evening. Then, one day, by chance, we bumped into her father on the street, and she turned pale. There must have been a very serious issue between them, I think he'd raped her, even though she never said so explicitly. She had no contact with him, but, as time went by, I realized just how present he was in her head, in her actions. She hated him and missed him at the same time, and, above all, she felt guilty, and nobody could make her see sense on that front. This inner conflict affected everything she did. She was constantly immersed in dilemma-ridden situations at work, in her personal relationships, that pained her and always left her facing impossible choices.

She finally decided to consult a psychologist, but the more therapy she had, the more her pain seemed to intensify. In the end, half the time I'd try to take her into my arms, she'd hit me. Then, one day, she announced that she wanted to put an end to our relationship. She wasn't made for happiness, that was her verdict. In the end, I'd only ever been a spectator of her internal struggle, and this experience reinforced my belief that there was nothing you could do for others, especially not change them. Consequently, it was important to choose your company very carefully.

"What kind of family do you have?" Emma asked.

"Excuse me?"

"What's your family like?"

I felt a kind of vertigo, so fleeting that, by the time I was aware of it, I'd recovered my balance.

"Are you alright?" she asked, worried.

"I'm fine."

"You didn't answer me."

"About my family? There's nothing much to say."

"Come on, try."

I sighed. "What do you want to know?"

"Do you see them?"

"They're both dead. My mother from cancer and my father from a malignant tumor."

"How old were you?"

"About thirty."

"A bit young to lose your parents, don't you think?"

"That's strange, coming from you."

She gave a hint of a smile. "And do you have any brothers or sisters?"

"Two sisters, but we're not in touch."

"And you don't think that's odd?"

"Not at all. We had nothing in common. Over time we drifted apart, that's all."

A truck veered into the parking lot. Its powerful headlights forced me to close my eyes and, when I reopened them, everything looked darker.

"You know, I don't mean to pry into your business," Emma said in a more intimate voice. "I just wanted to warn you. I'm used to living like this, but to someone who's a stranger to my family it can sometimes seem odd."

I nodded in agreement.

"We really should go," I insisted.

"Yes," she agreed this time.

2

Emma guided me through the city of Bordeaux, with which I wasn't very familiar. We bypassed the center and entered a residential area that ran alongside the botanical gardens.

"After my father's death, my mother bought a piece of land in order to build on it," Emma said. "She needed to start afresh."

I slowed down, and luckily there was a parking space outside the house she indicated. It was built in a strongly modern style in contrast with the traditional houses around it.

We walked across the garden, and I stood aside while Emma rang the bell. You could hear noise coming from inside. Not music but rather a household appliance, and it was probably because it was so loud that her mother didn't come to open the door.

Emma rummaged through her bag, found a bunch of house keys, and we entered the hallway, where an abandoned vacuum cleaner was making the racket from hell. Emma switched it off, then called her mother and, receiving no reply, went to look for her.

She was in the kitchen, scrubbing a cooktop with impressive energy, and was startled by the appearance of her daughter.

"Oh, you're here."

"Mom, what are you doing? It's two o'clock in the morning."

"The house is in such a state that—"

"What about Sylvain?"

"He left again."

"Left?"

"Yes. You just missed him."

Emma introduced me as a friend, and her mother proffered her hand so quickly that I didn't have time to meet her eye. She tried to resume her work, but Emma raised her voice.

"Will you stop, please!"

"Don't shout."

"You told me on the phone that he threatened to kill himself. I've traveled across France. Do you think you could perhaps tell me a little more?"

Her mother began to shake. She was a well-groomed woman, obviously well educated, as was apparent from the walls lined with books. She must have had a management position either in education or in the civil service, but at a moment like this she was no more than a frightened animal.

"He looked very calm, you know," she said faintly.

"He always is to begin with," Emma replied.

Her mother adjusted her necklace. She was dressed for going out, complete with earrings, which looked a little odd at this time of night.

"He brought me flowers."

"So he wanted something from you."

"Don't be cruel."

"I know him, that's all."

"He said he was going to take me to a restaurant. He decided to have a bath . . ."

Emma's mother suddenly stood up straight and put a hand to her temple.

"Oh, no, the bath!" she exclaimed.

Emma went up the stairs ahead of us. The bath tub was heavily overflowing onto the tiled floor and starting to flood the bedrooms.

"Oh, my God!" her mother cried.

"Go get me a pail and floor cloth—two if possible," Emma simply said.

She and I got down to work. We had to be quick because the rugs were soaked, and the water was seeping through everything. Her mother, who had remained at the bottom of the stairs, asked if we wanted a coffee.

"Later, Mom."

Emma would wipe the floor with the cloth, then I'd wring it into the pail which I emptied regularly. This way, we managed to limit the damage. Then we put the rugs out on the balcony, turned the armchairs upside down, and dried the parquet.

Her brother had left his bag at the foot of one of the beds, and I took care of it. The water had seeped through it and, in particular, had soiled a collection of *Rahan*, a comic strip that looked like a prehistoric variant of Tarzan. I opened the books to let them dry. On every page, this Stone Age superman, covered in protruding muscles, dominated animals and enemies alike with the help of a huge knife.

Apart from that, the bag contained boxes of medicines, dirty socks, a train ticket, and a sleeping bag in a terrible state that bore witness to a nomadic life.

Emma and I didn't exchange a single word during all this time. Once we'd tidied everything up, she took me to the bathroom and handed me a towel so that I could wash my hands.

"Thank you," she said with a hint of a smile.

We found her mother in the kitchen, perched on a stool. She was desperately looking for the coffee. "I can't understand. I was sure I had some."

Her cupboards were crammed with multiple stacks, which by some miracle stood balanced.

"Never mind, Mom," Emma said. "Where do you think he's gone?"

Her mother came down from the stool. Her expression was

evasive. "He was screaming in the corridor. He said he was going to kill himself."

"And apart from that?" Emma continued in a cold voice.

"He mentioned Séverine."

"Has he seen her again?"

"He spoke to her on the phone, and it was alright."

"It's always alright at a distance."

"He swore he'd stopped, you know."

"Stopped what?"

"The substances."

"By himself?"

"Yes."

Emma repressed a slight chuckle.

"Leave me some hope, please . . ."

"That's not what it's called," Emma said, correcting her. "In this case, it's an illusion."

"He's tried very hard and—"

"Did he threaten you—yes or no?"

"Yes."

Emma said nothing. Her mother had started cleaning the cooktop again.

"Did you give him money?" Emma asked.

"Yes."

"You have to stop giving in to him, Mom. He'll go into the clinic as soon as he's run out of options. It's a simple as that."

"I know . . ."

"You know, but you don't realize the consequences."

"He's my son . . ."

Emma was making a considerable effort to control herself. It was obvious from the way she put down her cup. "So he's gone to Séverine's?"

"He wanted to see her one last time."

"One last time?"

"Before he killed himself."

Emma looked for her cigarettes.

"I know you don't believe he wants to do it, but your father was—"

"Stop it!" Emma screamed and left the kitchen.

She had to smoke right now, or she'd explode. The front door slammed, and I stayed with her mother for a moment. I could only see her back and hear the sponge rubbing the cook-top. I wondered what it was like to live alone, with this tragedy, in such a large house, then I went to join Emma.

She was standing against a wall, smoking. She was staring into the night.

"Are you going to go looking for him?" I asked.

She let out a puff of smoke. "What else can I do?"

"I get the feeling you don't believe in all this suicide business."

"It's more complicated than that. My mother's crazy, but she's right about this. He could very well do the same as my father. They're the kind that try and provoke you."

"What do you mean?"

"My father didn't necessarily want to die. What he wanted above all was to defy my mother. Except that it went wrong."

There was a police siren in the distance, then nothing.

"You should go," Emma said.

"You'll never find him."

"It's O.K., I have a few ideas. Séverine. The places where he buys his drugs. Addicts aren't adventurous, you know. They follow a routine."

A car full of young people drove past us. Its windows were closed, and the radio was spitting rap.

"I'll go with you," I said.

She turned to me and frowned. "Why would you do that?"

"Because you're on foot, and it's late."

"What do you take me for? I'm not twelve."

"Yes, I know, but—"

THE BEST THING · 75

"What happened to your principles?"

"I'm not trying to interfere in your life. I'm just acting as your chauffeur. We'll drive around the city, either find him or not, then I'll bring you back, and we're done."

I looked at the empty street, at the houses with their closed blinds, and felt her eyes on me. The funniest thing was that I was questioning my motives the same way she was. Why didn't I just bolt there and then? It was the ideal moment. Her brother sounded like a weirdo with a boundless talent for harm. Going after him could lead us to all sorts of depravity. What was my true motive? Was I still trying to honor my debt? This theory seemed rather simplistic.

"In that case, I'll just tell my mother, and we'll go."

"O.K."

She went into the house, and I was left alone in the moonlight. Perhaps there was a less rational reason for my not leaving right away. I'd never met anyone like Emma Cassenti. It wasn't just because of the quality of her stroke or her expertise in service station flora. That's what was spectacular about it. It was also because of a few small details that baffled me. When we were stopping the flooding, I'd felt something very peculiar. We were on all fours, holding floor cloths, it was a dreadful situation, and yet I felt good being there with her, beyond any rationale. This young woman's father had committed suicide, her mother was clearly half-crazy, her brother seemed doomed to destruction, and as for me, that night I was a long way from my personal itinerary. However, and this HOW-EVER changed everything, I was with her. What was it about her that interested me so much? I heard the door open again.

"I'm ready," she said behind me.

Emma said all you had to do was drive along the River Garonne to reach the working class area where the said Séverine lived. With any luck, she was still at the same address.

"Do you mind if I roll myself a joint?" she asked.

"No, but open the window."

She had all she needed with her, and it all took very little time. Already, she was lighting the grass, and the smell spread through the passenger compartment.

"Do you smoke?"

"No."

"Do you disapprove?"

"No."

"Have you ever tried it?"

"Yes."

"Don't you like it?"

"Not really."

"I find it calming. It's more cocaine in the film industry, isn't it?"

"True."

"Do you use it?"

"No."

"Take the next right, we're nearly there."

I didn't take drugs, I didn't smoke, and I drank very little. It wasn't a question of morality or hygiene, even. Nor was it connected to the fact that I played sports, since, as we've recently discovered, many substances circulate in that allegedly healthy environment. It was simply that the idea of losing control wasn't something I found in the least exciting. Rightly or wrongly, I associated drugs with falling into a bottomless abyss, and I didn't like the idea of falling since it was bound to be painful.

"Turn right here," Emma said.

She indicated a narrow street, and we drove onto it at a reduced speed. She leaned her head out of the door, looking for a familiar building. "Here it is. You'd better stay in the car."

"Are you sure?"

"I'm certain. If he's there, he'll feel threatened, and that's the worst thing that can happen to him. And if he's not there, I don't suppose not meeting Séverine is something you'd miss out on."

She didn't give me time to reply and walked quickly toward the small, decrepit building. I waited a moment, then went the same way. I didn't want to follow her but wished to be at a safe distance where I could hear and react should the situation take a nasty turn.

The walls of the narrow corridor were peeling, and a simple look at the letterboxes gave you an idea of the precariousness of the residents. Some had been smashed, while others carried names that were crossed out or had become illegible. I sat at the bottom of the stairs while Emma's footsteps echoed up high. Séverine must have lived right under the roof.

The time switch went off, and now the corridor was only lit up by the street. Somewhere beyond the wall, an insomniac was watching a TV series of relative subtlety, judging by the regularity with which the dialogue was punctuated with bursts of machine-gun fire. I saw forms walk past furtively on the sidewalk—kids, judging by their size—wearing hoods. They were laughing and pushing one another, then their cheerful noises disappeared.

I thought of Cécile, and the way she looked at me in the bathroom mirror, and of Paul and the lucrative project he absolutely wanted to discuss with me. I remembered that when I was in school and played hooky, I'd go into buildings and sit on the stairs like this, so I could listen to life around me, ponder, and gather my thoughts.

Nothing happened for quite a long time, and I figured Emma was negotiating with her brother. From what I'd gathered, she was the younger of the two, and I wondered if Rahan had a sister and if he sometimes listened to her. I suddenly heard a metallic sound coming from the street. Faint, but regular enough to be intriguing, so I went to the top of the corridor without turning on the time switch. Damn it! It was the three kids! They were trying to take off one of the wheels of the Jaguar.

"Would you like some help?" I said.

The surprise effect was successful, and they flew away like sparrows. As I approached the car, I noticed that they'd left their tools behind: a makeshift jack, a wrench that was the wrong size, and a hammer. Still, they'd managed to remove two nuts, and I had to take the toolbox out of the trunk to put everything back. That's when Emma reappeared.

"What happened to you?" she asked.

"Nothing. Some kids trying to play a little trick. Well?"

"He came and left again, but I know where to find him."

I tightened the wheel once more with the wrench, and we left at full speed. We came across a police patrol car that ran a red light just ahead of us, and I nearly hit it. Then we crossed the River Garonne, which was very wide at this point.

"He kicked Séverine's door down and wrecked her apartment," Emma said. "Then he left. Séverine has taken refuge at her neighbour's, a little old lady who isn't afraid of young people."

"So how do you know where to find him now?"

"He was after dope. Séverine uses it, too. That's how they met. She told me about a place on the embankment where dealers conduct their business. Turn here."

I took the right turning, and we ended up on an esplanade right by the river and next to a park with benches, copses, and a laid-out avenue.

"She told me to look out for the statue," Emma said.

As we approached, two men walked away from a thicket, hand in hand. Several cars were parked, all with their lights off, but you could see that there were people inside. Emma asked me to speed up. She'd made out a shape in the distance.

"It's him," she said.

I slowed right down. Sylvain was average height and rather slender. In the dark, he could have been mistaken for a teenager. He turned into the park where another guy was waiting for him, a hand on his bicycle. Probably his dealer.

"Stop here," Emma said.

I switched off the headlights and let the engine run while she got out of the car. She took care to follow her brother at a distance but was soon in the open, and when the dealer saw her, he bolted. Dealers don't like surprises. Sylvain then turned around, and when he recognized his sister, he swore at her and started running as fast as he could.

I didn't know what to do. Wait for Emma or go after him? I chose the second option because I was afraid he'd get away from us, and this time for good. Of course, it was an uneven fight. I drove up to him, then, taking advantage of a cross street, I cut him off and leaped out of the car. He must have wondered who this guy coming out of the Jaguar was. He slowed down, stopped, trying to find a way to take off again, and suddenly burst out laughing, a bloodcurdling laugh, then headed straight for the embankment and threw himself into the Garonne.

It felt surreal. No, he hadn't! But he had. Emma was still far away, and my heart began to beat wildly. There was nothing poetic about it. It was reality with all the violence it can have at a certain time of night.

I ran to the embankment, hoping that Sylvain had played one of those tricks you see in the movies, when the fugitive pretends to jump but is actually hiding below the embankment, but, no, he was already in the Garonne, thrashing his arms in the water, calling me, provoking me. I took off my shoes and also jumped into the water.

It feels strange to plunge into the liquid element so brutally when a second earlier you were on dry land, in the realm of reason. I felt myself sinking into the murky water, which I didn't like very much, and started stroking vigorously to come back up. What was frightening was the feeling of heaviness. I weighed a ton, and it was as though my clothes were dragging me down. Every move was difficult, and it was a real struggle to stay afloat. In spite of everything, I managed to catch up with Emma's brother, who was swimming on the spot and still laughing.

"Hey, pal!" he exclaimed.

He really didn't look in a normal state of mind, but I proffered my hand, and as he smiled and let me come closer, I thought things would turn out well. That's when he hurled himself at me. One blow brushed me, but the other caught me straight in the temple, and I swallowed a mouthful of water. I was sinking and could see Sylvain getting away, when I felt a steady arm slide under my neck.

"Don't move!" Emma commanded.

I thought I was saved. I thought I was ridiculous. The two things at once.

"It's going to be O.K. Breathe."

I felt myself being carried away. Over there, on the bank, her brother was coming out of the water. He gave another crazy laugh, then vanished into the night.

Madame Cassenti was waiting outside the house. The police station had called her to say that a municipal patrol had nabbed her son. After receiving a generous load of threats and abuse, the police had thrown him into a drunk tank, and she was obviously relieved to know that his crazy flight had been stopped, and that he was protected from his demons, and possibly others from him.

"Would you like a little liquor?" she asked.

She was extraordinary, and yet I'd seen my fair share of "mother" specimens. Because of the stress and maybe also one of those pharmaceutical drugs that reduce anxiety, she had noticed nothing of our state and was only puzzled by the smell we gave off, which, she said, reminded her of "vacations." When the father was still alive, they must have gone on a family picnic by the river Garonne, and swum in it.

We went into the house. The vacuum cleaner had disappeared, but the living room rug was littered with hundreds of photos, since Emma's mother had gotten it into her head to "sort them out" there and then without wasting a second. Still, she was right, it was certainly time to bring some order into the family history.

Emma suggested I take a shower upstairs, while she'd use her mother's bathroom on the ground floor.

All I had brought with me, besides what I was wearing, was a track suit, and I remembered a series of skids on the hard-packed surface of the Tennis Club the previous day which made it in need of a wash. Emma promised to find me "something" to wear. Just as I was placing my foot on the first step of the staircase, she grabbed my arm. "Pay no attention to my mother, she's a bit high because of her pills."

"I gathered as much."

"I'm going to put her to bed."

I stood in the shower for a long time. The pungent smell of the Garonne gradually left me. I heard a knock. "I found you a robe," Emma said on the other side of the door. "I'm hanging it on the handle."

It was a collector's item, worthy of a government minister, that must have belonged to her father. It was too small for me, but at least it was dry.

By the time I came down, the atmosphere in the house had changed. Madame Cassenti was in bed, and Lauryn Hill's velvety voice, during her Fugees period, was filling the space while Emma melted chocolate in the kitchen.

"All this made me hungry," she said simply.

"So I see."

She refrained from commenting on my outfit, and for that I was grateful. As for her, she was wearing pajamas that made her look mischievous.

"Can you butter the bread?"

"Excuse me?"

She tasted the chocolate, then gradually, carefully added milk, making sure the mixture kept its creaminess.

"The bread's in the basket, the butter's in the fridge. Make sure you use the salted butter."

The drive, the stampede, the drowning, nothing was going to stop her from having breakfast in the middle of the night.

I sat at the counter that separated the kitchen from the dining room and began preparing generously-sized slices of bread with not too much or too little butter, the way she instructed, experiencing once again that feeling that had come over me during the flooding, a sense of calm in her presence. How could I possibly feel such well-being when, in less than twenty-four hours, she had slapped me, driven me to abandon a tennis game prematurely, and dragged me on a nocturnal race across the country that had led me to drink the bitter water of the Garonne? It was a mystery.

"Would you like a bowl of hot chocolate?" she asked, a glint in her eye.

"I'm not very hungry."

"Go on . . ."

"Alright then."

She sat on a stool opposite me.

She was beaming. She devoured at least four slices of bread and butter in a flash, and since she was dunking them in her hot chocolate, she kept having to stir. In the end, I don't know if it was because I kept looking at her, but I also got hungry, and we had to defrost some bread and make another pot full of hot chocolate. That was when she turned up the music, which wasn't loud enough for her, and started to dance on the tiles, barefoot.

"Don't worry about my mother. Once she's taken her pills, nothing can wake her."

She danced the way she swam. With such ease that it was almost indecent. I was there, on my stool, I knew I shouldn't look at her like that, but I couldn't help myself. She made a gesture for me to join her.

"Oh, it's not my kind of thing."

"Don't you ever dance?"

"Never."

"Really?"

"You know, at parties, the guy glued to the bar? That's me."

She burst into a crystal-clear laugh, and, before I had time to defend myself, she grabbed both my arms to impart a sway-ing movement to my entire body. There I was, in the middle of the kitchen, in that gold-trimmed robe that was too small for me. I thought I'd made a fool of myself in the Garonne, but that was nothing in comparison to what was going on now, and yet Emma wasn't making fun of me. She was trying hard, she genuinely wanted to initiate me into hip-hop rhythm as though it were the most important thing in the world, and, through sheer persuasion, I let myself go, my legs began to move of their own accord, independently of my reluctant brain, and I stared, dumbfounded, as though a spectator watching my own body become emancipated. Emma told me to make sure I didn't stop, then she let go of my hands, took a step away from me, and continued to dance for herself with her eyes shut, twirled, improvised, smiled blissfully, and only came back to me at the end of the song.

"See, you can dance," she simply remarked. "Come, let me show you something . . ."

What else was she going to do to me? Wasn't all this enough for one day?

She dragged me into the living room and kneeled down in the middle of the photo-covered floor. She seemed to be looking for one in particular, and finally found it. She handed it to me proudly. "Look at this . . ."

In the photo, there was a large number of people gathered around a garden table, having lunch in the sunshine. The table-cloth was white and the dishes plentiful, with children and adults sitting together. I took a closer look at the snapshot, which had lost some of its clarity over time. Some were raising their glasses, others were laughing, while others had their arms around each other, and every face gave out a feeling of communal celebration.

"That's me here," Emma said, pointing at a dark-haired, timid-looking little girl on her father's lap.

She took the photo out of my hand. It was as though it grew animated in her eyes, and the people in it were giving her a sign.

"I used to love these family celebrations," she said. "Sometimes there were fifty or a hundred of us, sometimes more. Cousins, young and old telling stories all at once. At the end, we'd put some music on and dance till we dropped. Afterwards, we'd play cards while others would sleep or chat in small groups. And, in the evening, everybody would sit at the table again and eat the leftovers. I thought that kind of life would never end . . ."

She looked for other photos while I looked at her. She was so much my exact opposite, it was fascinating. I'd been brought up in a tomb and she in a sunny garden. She had lived in the midst of a crowd of cousins and close relatives, while we didn't socialize with anybody and I'd had to climb over a wall to go and discover the living.

"So what happened to all of this?" I asked.

"When my father died, everything fell apart. Some people said my mother was responsible for his suicide, others that it was our—the children's—fault. Bad luck is like a disease, people are scared of catching it. Later, couples we thought indestructible split up, others died in a car crash, secrets came out of the drawers, and smiles gave way to payback. Life did its job, and, little by little, the table emptied. What I believed to be eternal turned out not to be."

A huge sadness came over her. Her face had altered, never had I seen anyone with such a changeable expression. You could see death in her features, and it almost frightened me. Then, all of a sudden, she snapped out of that past, and life started throbbing inside her again.

"What about you?" she said.

"Oh, well, me . . ."

"What was your childhood like? You're not going to let me do all the talking, are you?"

"I've told you it was nothing."

"There's no such thing as nothing."

"Yes, there is."

"Please . . ."

It was what—four in the morning? It didn't seem to matter to her. She'd opened a chink in time, a gap of freedom where everything was possible, and she was camping out in it, determined to use it to the full.

"Alright," I said. "I was in a waiting room, and one day I left. Happy?"

"Didn't you love your parents?"

"I don't know."

"You don't know?"

"Honestly. I had no reference point outside life in that house, and I found it rather strange, yet at the same time I didn't know what it was like in other people's homes . . ."

I was trying to put it simply, so it would take as little time as possible. "Try to picture," I continued, "the exact opposite of your crowded table and your laughter. No one ever laughed in our house, let alone danced. In any case, my parents didn't have time for it. My father worked in a factory, my mother at the market, then she'd sit at her sewing machine and make clothes she then sold. The person I saw most of was my grandmother, but she wasn't very chatty, and I was a little scared of her. She lived upstairs and almost never came down. My mother would go up to see her regularly, they had their ritual, doing the accounts, reading cards, then, gradually, she stopped going upstairs, and one day my grandmother hanged herself. So you see, I also have a someone who hanged herself."

Emma was hugging her knees and resting her chin on top of them. "How did she do it?"

"The hanging? She attached herself to a pipe but didn't get it right, the pipe snapped. She died all the same; just eight days later, her heart gave out."

I smiled in spite of myself. I'd never talked about any of this. I couldn't believe I'd done it.

"Why are you smiling?"

"Because I think it was the only time there was any life in that house. My mother made croque monsieurs. My father played Parcheesi with us. Any more, and I would have enjoyed death."

Emma said nothing and watched me. She was so close to me that I could hear her breathing.

She decided to show me other photos. I saw her on a little scooter, in the mountains, with a hat pulled over her eyes, at the beach with her already slender legs. Then, older, with her female friends, competing at pulling faces, wearing make-up for the first time. I saw her on a podium at a swimming championship. Standing in a wheelbarrow, in the middle of a recitation. At sixteen, with a boyfriend. Then I saw her parents in the kitchen, her mother smiling nervously and her father looking pensive while, sitting across the table, the children watched them, unaware of what was brewing. I also saw her grandmother in her vegetable garden, and Emma suddenly remembered a blueberry cake she'd vowed to try to make one day. I saw quite a lot of her life in just a few photos.

"This time I really am going to bed," I said.

"O.K., just one more cigarette."

I sighed, and she burst out laughing.

"Would you like some coffee?"

"No, thank you."

She returned from the kitchen with coffee and a cigarette, and sat on the couch. Something was puzzling her.

"Do you have any screenplays about this?"

"About what?"

"About your story."

"That's not what I do."

"I don't understand. Don't you write stories?"

"No. I doctor other people's screenplays."

"Haven't you ever wanted to write a screenplay of your own?"

"No."

"Why not?"

"I don't find it interesting."

She was drinking her coffee. She was looking at me.

"How about a novel? Have you thought of that?"

"Oh, that's totally not for me. You have to shut yourself away for months. It's not my kind of thing."

She was thinking. I must have been quite an oddball from where she was sitting.

"So what are you interested in?"

"What do you mean?"

"In life."

"Now that's a good question."

"Which you're not going to answer tonight . . ."

"Quite."

"It was kind of you to jump into the water for my brother's sake."

All of a sudden, she was a woman. I definitely had to go to bed.

"Even if I didn't manage to catch him," I replied.

The two of us were in this house, in this living room. It was very late. There was no more music.

"Which room am I sleeping in?"

"Take the one upstairs, on the right."

"Alright."

When I reached the top of the stairs, I glanced down. Emma was still looking at the photos, unable to leave them. She was stroking them with her finger, as though to bring all those faces to life for a little longer.

I went into the room. It overlooked the garden, and since it was a little windy, I pulled up the blind to see the trees sway. It was one of my favorite things, to watch the trees stirring before I went to sleep. I lay down on the bed.

I'd never told anyone about my grandmother's death.

Images flashed back in my memory. The wake, my father telling a story from his military service days, his sudden desire for onion soup, and my mother, whose feet couldn't reach the floor when she was sitting on a chair, my mother was so touching, that evening. Then, the next day, life had resumed its course, my father was sitting at the head of the table again, waiting to be served, and sent me back to the bathroom because I'd forgotten to wash my hands, my mother's soup was too salty and the announcers' skirts too short. Everything was back to the way it was before.

I lay there for a long time, eyes wide open in the darkness of the room. With Emma, nothing went back to the way it was before.

A Batman figurine was hanging right above me from the ceiling. It was spinning slightly, staring at me with its cruel little eyes. This must have been Sylvain's bedroom when he was still living in this house.

I had slept without interruptions and felt rested. I heard a kind of scraping, as though a piece of furniture was being shifted. I put on the robe and went out on the landing. I saw Emma's mother downstairs. She was holding a large wooden board with both hands and dragging it across the tiled floor. "Good morning!" she said cheerfully.

"Do you want some help?"

"Oh, it's all right, I'm used to managing on my own."

Even so, I went downstairs and lifted the board from the other side, if, for nothing else, to stop that dreadful noise.

"It's the extra leaf for the table. Emma's at the police station."

"Oh . . ."

"She spent almost an hour negotiating over the phone and managed to get her brother out on condition that he checks into this clinic near Toulouse. Are you aware that he's supposed to get treatment there?"

"Yes. Emma mentioned it."

"It's his birthday today."

"Whose?"

"My son Sylvain's."

I realized that the extra leaf was for the celebratory meal.

Emma's mother must have gotten the years mixed up and remembered those when the entire family used to get together. She, too, must have missed them.

"Besides, the police took that into account. When all's said and done, they're human, too. I hope you'll give us the pleasure of your company. It's very important for the atmosphere. I hope you like leg of lamb."

At that moment, I considered that she had cut her husband down from the ceiling of a first house before building another one. I know it's stupid, but I couldn't bring myself to say no to her. "I love it. Do you have Wi-Fi in the house?"

"Of course."

I went back to my room and put my computer on the bed. The Skype portal showed that a correspondent had tried to connect twice already, and I had no doubt it was Cécile. I clicked on Call, the ringtone started to buzz, and her face appeared. "I can't see you," she said a little abruptly.

I activated the camera option. Cécile squinted to take a better look at the place where I was staying. She was a little near-sighted but too vain to wear glasses. "What's that Batman behind you?"

"Don't worry about it."

"I've tried calling you twice already. I have a plane to catch and very little time."

"You're going away?"

"To Marbella. It's an amazing opportunity. You know I must do that interview with Erik . . . Erik Arlo. The guy you must absolutely work with. That's if you still plan to work . . ."

Obviously, she was talking about the genius, and I noted the dig aimed at me, but that was fair enough.

"He was at the Goshlin preview, which was excruciating, by the way, and we got on really well. He invited me to go with him to see Bredan Lamar—he wants her for his movie. Lamar has a villa in Marbella. So I can kill two birds with one stone, you see. Isn't it brilliant?"

"Yes."

She'd seen pictures of Lamar's villa in a magazine. She described it to me as a paradise. I wondered if she'd suddenly turned into a real estate agent. Having said that, the genius didn't lack a sense of politics. In fact, that was probably where his true talent lay. The interview would give substance to his project, though even in that case, Lamar, who was a real star reputed for being able to read a screenplay and recognize a good director, was still very far from agreeing to be in his movie.

"Now, you'd better tell me where you are, Antoine, and why. I couldn't make head or tails of your message AT ALL."

It was the moment of truth. I tried to focus in order to be clear and concise. "It's quite simple, I—"

That's when the bedroom door opened, and, before I could finish my sentence, Emma's brother made a triumphant entrance and collapsed onto the bed, right in front of the screen. "Hello! It's me!" he shouted.

I could see the incomprehension on Cécile's face.

"He saved me, you know!" he added. "Hey, are you his chick? What's your name?"

I tried to intervene, but Emma appeared in order to fetch her brother and grabbed him by the arm. "Come here, please," she said firmly.

"Alright, alright, I'm coming . . ."

Her brother didn't put up much of a fight. He was giggling, pleased with the achieved effect, and that was enough for him. Emma turned to me before leaving the room. "I'm sorry . . ."

I found myself face to face with Cécile, who was staring daggers at me.

"Who's that guy?"

"A boy with issues."

"That's rather obvious. And the girl?"

"His sister."

"What's your connection to these people, Antoine?"

Whenever her speech slowed down and she enunciated like that, it was a very bad omen. A symptom of cold, rising anger.

"It's very simple. What happened is that—"

Emma's mother then came into the room. She seemed very agitated.

"Yes?" I said.

"Sorry to bother you, but I wanted to warn you, don't worry if you see smoke, it's the oven. There's a slight problem with the settings. Emma's dealing with it now."

"Very well."

"I shan't bother you anymore."

"That's very kind of you, thank you."

I didn't make the slightest movement as the door closed. I knew Cécile was watching me and put off as long as I could the moment I'd meet her eye.

"Is Emma the young woman?" she said.

"Yes."

She came closer to the screen and examined all the corners of the room. She must have wondered if any other people were going to pop out, a large, naked black man, a dwarf dressed as Napoleon, that kind of attraction.

"What are you doing in these people's house, Antoine?" Her tone was extremely icy.

"It's very simple."

"You already said that."

"On the other hand, I'm not sure you have time to—"

"No, I don't. But I do have time to tell you that if you'd gotten back last night, you would have met Erik."

"I couldn't be there last night. I would have arrived in the middle of the night at the earliest."

"Don't treat me like an idiot. I spoke to Aurélien Belmer's assistant. I know you handed in your work yesterday morning. So I'm wondering what you could have been doing all this time instead of coming home . . ."

"I played tennis."

Cécile paused. This piece of information had to find its place on her scale of priorities, and it was way down at the bottom.

"Tennis, of course."

We both remained silent, each in front of his or her respective screen and the other's face, aware that this episode would leave marks. Then she grabbed her cell phone. She had a message.

"The cab's downstairs."

"Call me when you get there, and we can talk more easily," I said in a spirit of appeasement.

But Cécile wasn't the least interested in appeasement, at least not at this moment.

"You know, Antoine . . ."

"Yes."

"There are times in life when one has to make a choice."

"True."

I was happy to grant her this multi-purpose truth. She was wearing a piece of jewelry which dated from the time before we lived together. I really should have seen it as a sign.

"Take care," she added.

Then she disconnected, and I was left with a black screen, staring at the little symbol that informed me I was "disconnected." What annoyed me wasn't that Cécile was being judgemental—that I could accept—but the fact that at no point had I glimpsed the possibility of communicating with her about what was happening in my life in real time. Perhaps we would have laughed about it, extracted some goodness from it together. But there was nowhere for that between us. There was a cab waiting to sweep her off to a fabulous world out of the league of an amateur tennis player who couldn't tell a genius if he saw one. "You know, Antoine, one has to make a choice." I'd gone astray, that's all she needed to know, and I was going to be sorry.

A strong smell reached my nostrils. The oven, Emma's mother had mentioned the oven. I went out on the landing and froze. The entire house was filled with smoke. As I went down the stairs, I found myself surrounded by a fog that grabbed me by the throat and made my eyes sting. Through the wide open front door, I saw Emma, sitting on a chair she'd placed outside. She was engrossed in a manual, no doubt oven instructions, while in the kitchen, her mother was striving to wave away the smoke with a straw hat. All we needed to complete the tableau was her brother.

He suddenly emerged from the fog and took me in his arms.

"Oh, brother-in-law, please forgive me," he said in a sincere tone. "Sometimes I go a bit too far with my jokes . . ."

"I'm not your brother-in-law, Sylvain."

"Oh, but I thought . . ."

This didn't stop him from hugging me as tight as he could. There was great sincerity in his gesture, so much so that he was almost shaking, and, strange as it might seem, something inside me was moved.

That's when there was a muffled explosion and we all converged on the kitchen. The oven, either as a reaction to intense combustion or else by a mysterious effect of household electronics, had suddenly been flung open, and as we approached, we were able to assess what was left of the leg of lamb. The wretched thing had shrunk on the bone, and its flesh was no more than charcoaled remains.

"I'll take you out to eat," I said.

"Absolutely not!" the mother exclaimed.

"Yay! Some sauerkraut!" the son proclaimed.

I saw astonishment in Emma's face which equalled my own. I'd heard myself issue this invitation the way I had offered to drive her to Bordeaux when she was standing before me, her bag over her shoulder, at Menton station. Who did this voice belong to? To another me about whom I knew almost nothing.

We decided to shut all the windows overlooking the street and open wide those on the garden side. Other than that, going to the restaurant seemed like the least bad solution, at the stage I was at. Unless Emma's mother decided to visit the kitchens, we had every chance of an uneventful meal, with Rahan apparently having put away his huge knife. Besides, it's not as though an extra hour or so would have made a difference, now that Cécile was flying off to Southern Spain, to its dreamy swimming pools and synthetic fur-upholstered water beds. My cell phone vibrated. That's right, there was still Paul.

"Antoine?"

"Yes?"

"Are you in Paris?"

"Not quite."

"Meaning?"

6

Finding an Alsatian restaurant in Bordeaux wasn't exactly child's play. But it was Sylvain's birthday. We finally managed to find a brasserie removed from the city center, *La Taverne Munichoise,* which, according to internet reviews, served the best sauerkraut in the region. The information hadn't widely spread yet, or else it wasn't sauerkraut weather, because the place was almost empty. The waiter sat us by the impressive fireplace, and it took much persuading on the part of the head waiter to convince Sylvain that lighting a fire this time of year would be a bit excessive.

I went to wash my hands, and, as I looked up through the small window above the sink, I saw a field of crosses. The brasserie was adjacent to a cemetery.

Emma's mother couldn't have been happier. She was dressed for a wedding and kept praising everything, the weather, the restaurant decor, how polite the staff was, the shape of the glasses. After the waiter had taken our order, she launched into a story that dated back to the time when Sylvain and Emma were still children. They'd gone to Normandy for a weekend with a colleague of her husband's, his wife, and their children. They'd rented rooms in a hotel in Étretat, visited the region, and spent time on the beach. She remembered in particular a very happy picnic. Sylvain let her talk but was smiling somewhat mockingly, and, at one point, when he called the waiter, I saw Emma watching him intently.

"What?" he said to her.

"Nothing."

"Good sauerkraut without beer is a sin, isn't it?"

Emma didn't reply. She simply held his gaze until he burst into a slightly forced laugh.

His mother continued her trip down memory lane, totally oblivious to everything. As a happy closure to these days of relaxation, the two couples had treated themselves to an evening out without the children, at the local cinema. They'd seen *Roman Holiday,* and she still remembered Gregory Peck's saturnine aura.

"Be sure you tell us how it all turned out," Sylvain said suggestively.

Emma's mother had a coughing fit. She turned purple, and I thought it would never end. She tried to take a sip of water but upset her glass while attempting to pick it up. Sylvain looked at me mockingly.

"Dad's colleague wouldn't stop ogling my mother . . ."

"Where did you get this from?" she protested.

"In the end, my father was so livid, he blew his top in the car and hit the sidewalk, and unfortunately broke the wheel spindle, so we had to get back by train."

"There was gravel," his mother corrected between coughs.

"Yeah, right."

"You had no way of knowing, you were asleep. You were sunburned."

Sylvain started twirling his table knife in his hand, as his mother caught her breath.

"Are you having dessert?" Emma asked.

She was very calm on the surface, but I could sense she was on the alert. She was trying to catch her mother's eye to signal that it was time to change the subject.

"I'll have an opera cake," the mother said, adjusting her necklace. "I always have an opera cake."

Sylvain was talking to me again. "My baby sister is cool,

isn't she? I meant to ask you, brother-in-law, just how fast does your car go?"

"Sylvain," Emma said, "Antoine and I aren't together."

"No kidding?"

"The Jaguar's top speed is two hundred and thirty kilometers an hour," I said.

"I used to have a Merc. An SL coupe I bought second-hand. A super car. I could go up to two hundred and fifty. A real knockout!"

If memory served, the SL range had never gone beyond two hundred and twenty, but I took care not to correct him.

"I never saw ANYONE overtake me when I had that car. If anyone ever as much as tickled me, all I had to do was step on it a bit and, bingo, he'd become a dot in the rearview, minus the guy . . . And guess how long it took me from Nantes to Paris? Hey?"

I pretended to think but was observing Emma. She'd called the waiter to speed up the service.

"Come on, give me a number!" Sylvain said excitedly.

"Three hours."

"Two hours forty, pal."

"That's very fast."

"And that's with taking my foot off for the speed cameras. But fucking hell, I had to sell it."

"You mean the bailiff seized it," Emma slipped in.

"It was that idiot from Tax. Fucking inspector. I should have made him swallow his tongue . . ."

Sylvain grabbed his glass and drained it in one go. I caught Emma's eye, warning me that the friendly family meal was about to go downhill. It was just a matter of time.

"Nothing for me," I said to the waiter.

It was at that moment that the mother decided to take a package tied with ribbons out of her shopping bag. She really did have an acute sense of observation.

"A birthday without a present is not a birthday," she said.

"Let's do this at home, mom," Emma suggested.

"Really?"

"Hey, you, you're not laying down the law," Sylvain replied. "Come on, Mom, give it here!"

I stood up.

"And what are you doing?" Sylvain asked.

"I'll be back."

"Oh, you're going to pay, yeah, go pay, you've got dough, it's obvious."

He'd only had one and a half glasses, but the alcohol was taking over his cells.

I went up to the till and asked the owner for the check. She gave me a worried look, but I reassured her that the food was excellent, so was the service, but we were in a rush. It took what felt like ages for her to sort out the bill, and I gave her my card, thinking that we'd get away without any damage, but that's when there was a loud crash in the dining area.

Sylvain had knocked over the table, and the waiters were chasing after him. They were trying to trap him at the far end of the restaurant, but he'd gotten hold of a knife and was keeping them at bay. His mother had fallen backwards, and Emma was in the process of picking her up.

"We were having such a nice time," I heard her mother whisper.

I don't know if it was because of his heroic-prehistoric reading, but Sylvain was very agile. Just when the staff thought they'd neutralized him, he threw the knife at them and, the instant they stepped back, leaped to another part of the room and opened the window. He was out in a flash.

"What happened?" I asked Emma.

"It's the present," she replied, pointing at the floor.

I looked down. There was a splendid box of oil paints, totally gutted, tubes scattered, brushes all over the place, and it was clear that Sylvain couldn't stand this rather too explicit request that he go back to being a good boy whose mom could be proud of him.

I gave the waiter a few bills to cover the breakage and went toward the exit.

"What are you doing?" Emma said.

"I'm going after him."

I wasn't sure I could bring him back with me, but I felt I had to try. He was also the kid who had taken me in his arms amidst the smoke from the leg of lamb.

It was when I reached the boulevard that I realized the presumption of my plan. Sylvain had vanished into thin air, and there wasn't even a passer-by I could ask which direction he'd taken.

I walked alongside the cemetery, then went in, thinking that he had perhaps done the same. In these circumstances, it was better to follow one's instinct.

I walked at random down well-kept paths and patrolled the graves until I reached a wealthier area where family tombs were concentrated. And, suddenly, I saw him. He was curled up at the foot of a cross erected on a kind of plot. He was crying. I sat next to him and put my hand on his shoulder. A spasm shook his entire body.

"It'll be alright," I said.

"No, it won't."

"Yes, it will . . ."

"I'm scared, if only you knew how scared I am . . ."

"Of what?"

"Of everything."

He was holding his head in his hands, staring at the ground.

"Weren't you supposed to go into a clinic?"

"Yes."

"Why don't you go?"

"I'm telling you I'm scared."

"Emma and I could take you there."

"What?"

"We could take you to the clinic."

If memory served, it was somewhere near Toulouse, so less than an hour's drive from Bordeaux. At this point, it didn't make a huge difference to me.

"What do you say?" I continued. "It would be a nice drive . . ."

He was overwhelmed by another bout of tears. I noticed that his knee was bleeding. He must have scraped it jumping through the window. He raised his head a little.

"Alright, but on one condition. You let me drive your car."

I'd never lent my Jaguar to anybody. It wasn't a matter of possession. I'd always found subscribers to "my house, my car, my wife" ridiculous. No, my reticence had to do with driving. Let's face it, most people aren't in control of their vehicles; it's not their fault, the driving license is a joke.

When I worked for the magazine devoted to sports cars, where I tweaked the texts, I was entitled to a driving training session in a single-seater on the Castelet racetrack. That's where I got to understand about trajectory, learned to take into account the transfer of weight when braking and accelerating, and also all the details that ensure safe driving: the way of adjusting your seat much closer to the dash than people usually do, of holding the wheel so you keep your arms relaxed and can swerve at any moment, to build up speed gradually. I came back from the training session a much better driver. That's why I hate sitting in the passenger seat, especially in a fast car, because I know perfectly well that if there's an accident, the self-confident, domineering driver will invariably make the wrong decision, brake abruptly, and turn the wheel in every direction until he loses hold of the road, instead of speeding up gradually and remaining lucid.

"All right," I nevertheless replied.

It went against all prudence, in total opposition to my way of thinking, but I felt it was the only chance, however childish, of restoring his self-confidence.

"Really? You'd lend it to me?"

"Yes."

"That's so cool."

All of a sudden, he'd forgotten everything, the table knocked over, the damned weekend in Étretat, his hatred. At that moment, the cave man had found himself a brother, and I wondered if he was going to suggest we exchange a blood oath. As things stood, I probably would have gone along with it.

"Still, it was really good sauerkraut," he said.

The sky was black above the cross. It was too hot to last, and there was a rumble of thunder.

"Don't you think the meat was a little tough?" I asked.

"No, I quite like it like that," Sylvain replied. "But they could have given us more sausages."

7

Emma nursed her brother's knee while her mother went to get him some pants. She brought back several pairs that must have dated back to his teenage years but still fit him perfectly, as though his body had decided to stop growing at that time.

I waited in the living room, which looked out onto the garden. On the coffee table, there were magazines and a stack of books. One title drew my attention: *The Power to Change,* by Vladimir Robowski. It was an essay on behavioral psychology, and the headings asked questions about the human ability to evolve. Does accepting what we are prove we're opposed to change? Is there a difference between judgement and understanding? Does growing up imply abandoning a part of ourselves? Reading the summary on the back cover, I discovered that Robowski, whose work had triggered many imitators, especially in the United States, had committed suicide in 1975. I hoped it wasn't by hanging.

Possibly in order to come to terms more easily with our departure, Emma's mother had started cleaning again. The cremation of the leg of lamb had coated the walls in a layer of fat she was now tackling, equipped with sponge and stool. For all Emma's telling her to leave this chore to the cleaning lady, she wouldn't listen.

"Stop treating me like an old woman," she protested, nearly falling off her perch.

She walked us to the car and, when she kissed me goodbye,

I sensed just how tense she was. I'd been at her place for almost twenty-four hours and still not made eye contact with her. I thought of Robowski's psychology book and figured she must have acted in life the same way she had with the oven manual. She carefully read the instructions but, when it came down to it, pushed the wrong buttons.

Emma sat at the back and Sylvain behind the steering wheel. I gave him the basic guidelines, and he looked eager to start driving. He made the six cylinders roar and smiled like a child. You'd have thought that taking this trip at the controls of the Jaguar constituted his real birthday present. He took care not to brutalize the clutch, and the car started gently, with a soft growl.

I turned to look at their mother. She seemed tiny on the sidewalk, and as we drove away, she waved at us. It was as though we were leaving for summer vacation. In spite of all the tragedies they'd been through together, there was something more real between them than anything I'd experienced in my family. I found their madness human, whereas my parents' normality seemed like pure heresy.

Sylvain felt at home in Bordeaux and reached the highway junction easily. Against all expectations, he drove well. I thought he'd want to prove he was a real racing driver, the way almost all males do when behind the wheel of a sports car, but no, he handled the Jaguar level-headedly and even with a degree of subtlety. Once we were on the highway, he asked if this model had a "cruise control" function, I said yes, and he used it to settle comfortably at a hundred and thirty kilometers an hour. All he wanted, he said, was to have a bit of a drive, and he looked like he meant it.

Emma asked if we could stop at the next highway station so she could buy some marshmallows, and a childhood scent filled the car as they both began chewing their sweets. We resumed our journey without delay, and Emma leaned between our seats, her head resting just behind me, and I felt she was happy.

Sylvain had fun listing all the times his mother had ruined a meal when friends of his parents or relatives were expected, because of her very personal sense of cooking time. He was capable of a sharp sense of humor when he wasn't under the influence of a substance, and knew how to exploit the comic element inherent in these situations. His mother was "absent-minded" but had always fought against this trait, and it was precisely her attempt to avoid these blunders that increased her chances of making them. For example, by marinating fish a long time ahead but using engine oil, or by setting the oven in such a way that cooking had no possibility of actually starting. What was funny wasn't so much her clumsiness but the fact that she'd done her best to avoid it. Her talents didn't apply only to the culinary arts, however. She'd regularly forget to put the handbrake on in her car and then find it lower down the street, or else kept the gas turned on. All these stories had something in common, in that none of her slips had ever triggered a real drama, as she always pointed out whenever the people close to her poked fun at her. Obviously, her husband's suicide and her son's addiction did not feature on that list.

The clinic was in the middle of the countryside. We left the highway just before Toulouse and took a secondary road across some vineyards. We'd left the thunderstorm behind us, and the sky was now cloudless. It was a beautiful day. When the road started winding, I suggested to Emma's brother that I drive, since this section required more technique. Something else I had learned on the racetracks. Euphoria often goes together with falling, and it's precisely when everything is going like a treat that you must be twice as prudent.

I expected Sylvain to be a little offended by what he could

have interpreted as a lack of trust on my part, but that wasn't the case. He was more and more relaxed. He glanced at his sister in the rear view mirror and asked if she remembered a song they'd sung at the top of their lungs on the way back from vacations in Spain. "Nantes," by Barbara. Apparently, it was a custom that they sang in the car, and the repertoire of the lady in black had lulled many trips. Brother and sister began to sing "Nantes" with a touch of irony but with a thorough knowledge of the tune and the lyrics.

> *Vingt-cinq rue de la Grange-au-Loup*
> *Je m'en souviens du rendez-vous*
> *Et j'ai gravé dans ma mémoire*
> *Cette chambre au fond du couloir . . .*[1]

I found their ability to laugh at the events in their lives and turn them into a performance quite surprising.

> *Au chemin qui longe la mer*
> *Couché dans le jardin de pierre*
> *Je veux que tranquille il repose*
> *Je l'ai couché dessous les roses*
> *Mon père, mon père . . .*[2]

Once again, this was the exact opposite of what I'd lived through. In the Cassenti household, life's tribulations, grief included, could be lived out in the open, whereas in my family every event had been covered with a leaden weight.

---

[1] *Twenty-five, Rue de la Grange-au-Loup / I remember the rendezvous / And I have, etched in my memory, / That room at the end of the corridor . . .*
[2] *On the path along the sea / Lying in the stone garden / I want him to rest in peace / I lay him down beneath the roses / My father, my father . . .*

Was that why they expressed their emotions so freely? Whether it was through violence, in the brother's case, or through imagination, in the sister's? I was inclined to believe that was the case. In their eyes, you could flick out a knife or take a dance step at any time. All that mattered was the intensity and truthfulness of the moment. Life was a constant improvisation, while in my case everything had to be assessed and prepared before being experienced.

By now the road was snaking along the side of the hill, and the view was splendid. As we covered kilometers, a kind of osmosis had taken place inside the car. I could hear Emma's breathing, close to me, and her brother's childlike excitement. The three of us were there like kids off on a wander, and I had a general feeling that I was closer to them than to any other family I'd known till then.

That's when a Mercedes 4x4 appeared in the rearview mirror. It came up behind us very quickly, and I thought that, in its momentum, it was going to overtake us, but it didn't. It stuck to my bumper, and, to make it clear that I wasn't driving fast enough for it, deployed the full array of the perfect imbecile behind the wheel—flashing headlights, tooting horn, and obscene gesture.

"Look at that jerk!" Sylvain grumbled.

"Leave it," I said.

I wasn't going to let that idiot spoil such a beautiful day. I put my right turn signal on to let the hot-headed driver know that I was happy to let him through, and pulled over as far as I could. No use. The 4x4 remained behind us for another several hundred meters, as though inviting him to overtake us by making it easier for him was some kind of provocation. He finally made up his mind, and I heard him discharge the full fury of his V8, but he overtook us so randomly that I had to brush the slope to avoid his scraping the Jaguar.

Give it three bends, and I'll have forgotten all about you, I thought, but that's when the situation really deteriorated. Instead of driving away, the 4x4 slowed down to the point of forcing me to brake, sped up abruptly, then slowed down again.

"What's he playing at?" Sylvain squealed.

The cheerful expression on Emma's brother's face had given way to a markedly more belligerent grimace, and I realized I had to make a decision. The time for pop songs was over, Rahan could wake up any minute now because of that idiot, and God only knew what Sylvain would attempt to do in the heat of the moment, maybe climb on the roof of the Jaguar and leap onto the other vehicle with his large knife.

The 4x4 was now going at a steady speed, and the driver was examining me in his rearview mirror. He was looking out for a reaction on my part. This much was obvious, and I was doing my best not to have one, as a basic rule in this kind of situation. At this stage, I had only two choices. Either stop and let him go, or overtake him by surprise, but, in any case, I couldn't stay behind him. There was no way of knowing what kind of psychopath I was dealing with. Stopping, however, carried the risk of his waiting for me further along and the situation degenerating, especially with Sylvain next to me. So I opted to overtake him, and, once I thought I was close enough and had allowed the driver to drop his guard sufficiently, I shifted into a higher gear, sped up abruptly, and pulled out.

The Jaguar took a leap forward, and I found myself side by side with the 4x4 in what in car racing they call the zone of uncertainty, in other words in a position where you can outflank your adversary but equally be at his mercy. It happens all the time in competitions, when it's necessary to take a calculated risk, otherwise you just suffer, except that here we were on a secondary road and not a racetrack, with—to top it all off—a born idiot trying to mark his territory.

I suddenly had an overwhelming feeling. Call it instinct or experience, as you wish. I felt things would not turn out well. And, as a matter of fact, the large 4x4 kept up with my speed and gradually deviated from its trajectory. In an instant, I saw the driver's face. Strangely, he looked nothing like a madman behind the wheel, but rather like a high-ranking bank employee or civil servant. What had happened to him that day to give him the urge to reign over this country road like that to the point where he wanted to exclude me from it? I'll never know.

This time, it wasn't just the wheel of the Jaguar that scraped the embankment, but the whole car that quit the asphalt and went into the vineyard. I wanted to think I was dreaming, but the blood-curdling lament that rose from the coupe's guts as it churned the side of the hill left no room for doubt. We had definitely left the road. Nevertheless, I forced myself to put things into perspective. All three of us had our seat belts fastened, and the XJ model, in terms of structure, was supposed to be one of the safest. I then realized how sensible I'd been to take the wheel from Emma's brother. If I hadn't done it, I would no doubt automatically have thought myself capable of reacting better than him in these circumstances. And he would inevitably have felt responsible. We could count ourselves lucky that we'd escaped a grim situation.

We drifted like this for a dozen meters or so, gently, and I thought we'd get away with some crumpled bodywork and an injury to our pride. Until I saw the rock. What was that block of granite doing there in the middle of a vineyard? It seemed to have dropped out of the sky. Couldn't the owner of the vineyard have shifted it? And yet it took up a good dozen feet! What a mess.

From the way the Jaguar was sliding, its side was about to collide with the rock, at the level of my door. I'd be hit, of course, but my passengers would be unharmed. I thought at least that was something and wondered if the Jaguar was equipped with lateral airbags.

PART THREE
THE INSUBORDINATE ONE

1

When I came to, I was in a hospital room. I tried sitting up and wriggling my toes. Apparently, my body was all in one piece and seemed to be in good working order. I turned my head, and two things caught my attention on the night table. A drawing of a tree, with the dedication "To my dear brother-in-law," and a copy of Jean Anouilh's *Antigone*. From that I deduced that brother and sister had brought me here. Was that before they left? No idea. I remembered the rock, the noise of the iron churning up the vines, that was all.

I found the assistance button and pressed it. Shortly afterwards, the duty nurse came in.

"And that's what they call sleeping around the clock," she said.

She was short and plump, with a nice smile and lively eyes.

"Can I ask where I am?"

"At the Toulouse University hospital. Do you remember having an accident?"

"Yes, very clearly. How are the other passengers?"

"I only saw one. A young lady, and she was unhurt."

She checked the monitors as she spoke to me.

"Is she still here?" I asked.

"She sat with you until the gentleman from Paris arrived."

"The gentleman—oh, of course."

I realized it must be Paul. She took hold of my arm to check my blood pressure.

"Did I sleep long?"

"I just told you, twenty-four hours. You have a mild con-cussion, but the tests haven't shown anything terrible. More than anything else, you seemed very tired, so we decided to let you catch up on your sleep. Get up so we can have a look."

I sat on the edge of the bed and put my weight on my legs without difficulty.

"No dizziness?"

"No. The gentleman . . . do you know where he is now?"

"He went out into the corridor to make a phone call."

Only then did I realize that I was wearing pajamas and that there were sandals under the night table.

"Can I go out and walk a little?"

"It's even recommended."

"I feel slightly euphoric. Is that normal?"

"Well, we did drug you a little, so avoid driving for the next few hours. Other than that, unless you faint in the grounds, you're ready to be discharged."

In the corridor, a cleaner was mopping the floor. There was a smell of bleach.

Paul was really there. He'd found a bench, slightly apart. Planner on his lap, phone against his ear, he was juggling his appointments. However, as soon as he saw me, he cut the con-versation short and came toward me, his face very serious.

"How are you feeling?" he asked.

"Very well. You really didn't have to come all the way here, Paul."

"No, you can't say that. Remember I'm your emergency con-tact."

He was right. I suddenly remembered that his was the name I wrote down on administration forms. Living with Cécile had changed nothing. Actually, should I let her know? Given the success of our Skype conversation in Bordeaux, I couldn't see myself telling her I'd had an accident in the company of the same people, on the way to a health center for addicts.

"Besides, I've got some papers for you to sign," Paul continued. "And there's that job offer I really want to discuss with you."

"So then it's a professional visit."

"Definitely."

We both knew that wasn't true. Paul would get insanely worried if anyone close to him was admitted to the hospital. And his mother's death hadn't helped on that front.

"I saw her, you know," he said.

"Who?"

"The person who stopped you going home . . ."

I was determined to talk about Emma as little as possible. Even with Paul.

"The nurse suggests I go out for a walk," I said, cutting him short. "Come with me. By the way, thanks for the pajamas."

"It wasn't me who brought them."

There were tables and chairs arranged in the arcades that framed the grounds. We sat there, and I pictured Emma choosing pajamas for me, trying to work out my size. Paul was watching me.

"What?" I said in the end.

"Am I allowed to ask if there's something going on in your love life?"

"Definitely not."

"I'm not allowed?"

"Well, of course you are, but, no, nothing's going on."

Paul waited a beat, as though to materialize the separation between the personal and the professional world, then opened his bag.

"So Belmer had a stroke when he realized Carole was sleeping with Roman Tosik."

"She's sleeping with Roman? I thought she hated him."

"She hates losing. It was the only way she could get back into the game."

"Funny. I never would have thought she was Belmer's type."

"In any case, he's resting now, and his wife has taken control of the production. In other words, there are now fewer helicopters and more accountants. She doesn't understand anything about what she calls our 'arrangement.' She thinks you're paid too much for a consultant and not enough for a screenwriter."

"You know I'm neither one nor the other."

"I told her that. Anyway, she's not challenging her husband's decision, but she wants more guarantees."

"Where do I sign?"

"You don't have to if you think it's going too far. We can ask her to—"

"We'll ask her nothing," I said, interrupting him. "Give me a pen."

It was like a treaty between America and Russia. The document must have been a hundred pages at least and probably even took earthquakes into consideration.

"Now tell me about the contract of the century," I said, starting to initial the pages.

Paul suddenly livened up. Paramount wanted to do a remake of *Casablanca.* In a different geographical and historical context, obviously. Half of Hollywood had come up with screenplays, and they'd all ended up in the trash can. As a last resort, they'd issued a call in Europe, and, amazingly enough, I was on their list.

"How is this possible, seeing that I don't exist?"

"Delgado mentioned you."

Oscar Delgado was a hooligan. A real one. But also a much sought-after actor because of his distinctive face. He came from a world where people were killed for five hundred dollars, sometimes less. He frequented the underworld and was quite happy to threaten directors when he couldn't obtain from them what he expected, but, other than that, he was a desperate, very interesting man. He read Seneca and claimed that there was nothing more modern, though he didn't show off his culture and was caring towards others, something very rare in his profession. I was glad to help him back to his hotel, two or three times, when he was dead drunk.

"What do they want?" I asked.

"A strong idea. If it engages them, then a treatment."

"Who'd play Bogart?"

At that moment, I noticed Emma in the distance. She was wearing a lemon-yellow dress that really suited her. She wasn't alone.

"DiCaprio."

"And Bergman?"

"Johansson. You're unlikely to get this kind of opportunity very often . . ."

They were approaching. The man had a bandage on his forehead and a kind of loose-woven hat over his entire skull. He was tall, heavily built, with deeply-sunk eyes. Paul noticed I'd lost the thread of the conversation and looked in the same direction as me to see what was distracting my attention.

"Who's he?" he asked.

"No idea."

Emma came straight up to me. She was smiling. You would never have guessed that she'd come out of a car accident just twenty-four hours earlier. She walked around the table, put a hand on my shoulder, and kissed me on the mouth.

"Are you alright, darling?" she said, perfectly naturally.

I froze, unable to reply and making sure I avoided Paul's eye. He must have been waiting with a certain degree of curiosity to see what would happen next.

Emma turned to the man next to her. "This is Reinhart Zoll, the theater director, and this is Antoine, my partner. And Monsieur—"

"Paul Marquais. Antoine's agent."

"Marquais—I knew your mother very well!" Zoll said immediately.

"Really?"

While they were exchanging pleasantries, I tried to get a sign from Emma, but she simply smiled at me as though the situation were perfectly normal.

"It's providence, you know!" Zoll exclaimed.

"We met in the hospital lobby this morning," Emma said, "as he was going to ER. I've known Reinhart since drama school. He was one of my teachers."

"The first time I saw her, I thought *Antigone!*" he said. "Now, as it happens, I'm staging Anouilh's play as we speak, and I've lost my leading lady."

"Pull up a chair," Paul said, as polite as ever.

"Reinhart can't stay, unfortunately," Emma said hastily. She clearly didn't want for this situation to go on much longer.

"That's right," he said, as confirmation. "I must sort out some logistical problems and tell the company manager about Emma, but it's just a formality—the part is hers!"

Emma put a hand on my arm, and I nearly jumped.

"I'll just see Reinhart out, and I'll be back."

I watched them walk away. Perhaps I was in a coma and would wake up.

"So nothing's going on," Paul said.

"Surely you see it's an act."

"Then she's a very good actress, and you're right to be interested in her career."

"Are you done?"

"You're right, it's none of my business. Going back to *Casablanca*, I've brought you the screenplay that came closest to a favorable decision. It's by David Pachett, after all."

"What?"

"Remember—*Casablanca*?"

I suddenly felt slightly dizzy, like at the highway station, and it had nothing to do with the accident. She'd kissed me, called me darling.

"Maybe you'd like to have a rest?"

"No. Give me the screenplay."

It was very thick. At least a hundred fifty pages, which was unusual for an American screenplay. Paul made sure that I'd signed Madame Belmer's contract and initialed all the pages, then checked the time. He'd booked a seat on the afternoon plane. The evening one was full. He had to leave.

"I'll call you as soon as I've read it," I promised.

"Take care of yourself," he said, standing up.

I stayed alone at the table, under the arcades, and picked up Pachett's screenplay. It's only by doing something concrete that I'd manage to go back to my own life. All this was no more than an enchanted interlude, it was coming to an end, and as soon as I was out of this hospital, I'd have to be back on my way. I'd rent a car or take a train if the planes were all booked up. What mattered was that I remove myself from Emma and get back into my stride.

I was about to start reading when a brightly-colored dot on the horizon of tall trees caught my attention. Emma was already coming back. Good God, she was beautiful. She sat opposite me, and I pushed my chair back a little, as though afraid she would kiss me again.

"I owe you an explanation," she said.

"Yes, I think you do."

"Reinhart is a very good director. This part is more than I could ever have hoped for."

"That much I gathered."

"The problem is he's a sex maniac. Several fellow actresses have been victims of his actions. He never gives up. And if he feels he can't reach his ends, he fires us. It's what happened to the girl who was playing the part. Why do you think he has that bandage on his forehead? He said he ran into a beam, part of the scenery, but that's not true. It's because the girl put up a fight."

"How do you know?"

"I called her when he went in to be treated. We were together at drama school. I think she made two mistakes. She didn't sign a contract, and she didn't put an obstacle between herself and Reinhart."

"And I'd be your obstacle?"

"Marriage is the only thing he respects. He won't touch a married woman, or even one who's just engaged."

I thought I was going to choke.

"You told him we were married?"

"Only engaged."

"How nice of you to let me be free for a little longer."

She drew a breath.

"Please stay with me until I sign my contract. I'm seeing the company manager tomorrow, for sure. Then all you have to do is say you'll come back to see me, and let that possibility linger. With a contract and the threat of your return, I'll be able to keep him at bay. And I'll get my hours."

"Here we go again."

Her hours, of course, that was the real issue. They'd made her slap me and justified my need to make amends. They'd made me drive across France, swim in the Garonne, explore cemeteries and vineyards. And now chance, or fate, or call it what you will, had led this sex maniac from beyond the Rhine to get himself sewed up in this very hospital, thereby providing Emma and me with the opportunity to settle our accounts. However, I had to resist. There was no knowing where this new adventure would lead me.

"No," I said firmly.

"What do you mean—no?"

"No, I won't play the fiancé, or represent the threat. I'm going back to Paris. Don't you think I've done enough? I think I have."

Emma remained impassive.

"Is that your final answer?"

"Yes."

There was a moment of silence. It was lunchtime, and the grounds were deserted.

"So did your brother go to the clinic?" I asked.

"Yes. The gendarmes offered to drive us there. They were very kind."

"He went there flanked by two cops?"

"Yes."

"Very funny."

"You know, I'm sorry . . ."

"Why?"

"Your car . . ."

"Forget it. It was my decision to overtake him."

"If you hadn't taken this trip . . ."

"Emma . . ."

"Yes?"

"I really must go back."

She was opposite me. She looked serious, but her face didn't express anything excessive. There was sadness in her eyes, yes, you could see that, but not intently so. She was behaving in a dignified, modest way, and even managed a faint smile to answer me.

"I understand," she finally said.

"I understand"—what a horrible reply. I felt a knife slowly go into me and reach my heart. "I understand." I was ready to resist whole armies, confident in my common sense, in my arguments. I was determined not to give any ground. "I understand." I had all my reasoning, my words ready to fight, my foot soldiers, my cannons, in store. I was ready to face her fury, her contempt or her laughter, even her cruelty, anything she wanted. I would resist. But I hadn't expected her understanding.

2

I picked up my test results. They confirmed that everything was alright, and I filled in the administrative forms. Zoll had suggested picking Emma up in the early afternoon, so she and I had all the time we needed to establish a clear strategy before I agreed to play a part in this comedy. It would not last any longer than twenty-four hours. As soon as we got to the theater, her absolute priority would be to find the company manager and sign her contract. Afterwards, I'd say I urgently needed to return to Paris and that I would be back as soon as possible, so that the threat I was supposed to represent would linger.

When the theater director's car drove up outside the hospital, Emma slipped her arm under mine, and I tensed up.

"Don't overdo it," I said.

Zoll didn't bat an eyelid when he saw that I was coming, too, and asked Emma to sit in the front. We hadn't even gone ten meters before he started hitting on her.

"Béatrice Renzi told me all about you," he said, leaning toward Emma. "She saw you in the production of *Phèdre* directed by Michaud. Apparently you were extraordinary."

"We never got paid, but, yes, it was good," Emma replied, laconic.

"Have you at least made your hours?"

"Almost."

I liked the subtlety. Zoll, on the other hand, didn't have any. I'd seldom seen anyone drive so badly. He kept slipping the clutch, wouldn't ease the pressure from the pedal after braking, had no sense of the space around him, and, of course, would get angry with other drivers, unaware that he was constantly creating situations of uncertainty and challenge.

"I've often thought of you, you know," he carried on in a crooning voice, "including for this part, but I didn't know how to contact you. Do you still not have an agent?"

"No."

"You really need one, Emma," he said abruptly as he assessed her as potential prey.

She sighed. "I know."

Then she moved in such a way as to include me in the conversation space, and Zoll understood the message very well and interpreted it his own way. He moved to phase two of his attack, and tested the reality of our relationship.

"How did you two meet?" he asked.

"At a shoot," Emma replied, without turning a hair.

"We also had occasion to play tennis together," I said, gilding the lily. "Her backhand is her main weapon, a real slap."

Emma couldn't help bursting out laughing, and Zoll must have thought there was too much intimacy between us. He adjusted the rearview mirror and embarked on phase three: discrediting me.

"What's your surname again?"

"Maupas."

"Emma said you're a screenwriter . . ."

"A script doctor, actually."

"What's the difference?"

"I intervene when needed. I'm not involved in the overall writing process."

"So you're a repair man."

"You could say that."

On court, when you see this kind of adversary arrive, you

know the match is over before you've even taken out your racket. If anything, it's too easy. Self-importance is the mother of defeat.

"Antigone and the repairman," he said mockingly. "Pretty improbable."

"That's what I'm trying to tell her," I replied, looking Emma in the eye, "but she won't listen to me."

Her arm on the back of the seat, she held my gaze. She had kissed me. It was just play acting, but I had a right to remember some things, even if they were the result of fleeting circumstances and wouldn't lead anywhere.

Zoll bullied his way into a traffic circle, and the driver who was already in it panicked, but he didn't even notice. I wondered if it was much farther to the theater. Now he was glued to the bumper of a van, so that he couldn't possibly see what was going on in front.

"I've nothing against the cinema, but you must admit that it's not an art, or rarely is . . ."

It was like background music. Emma sat facing the road again, and I could look at the nape of her neck. Her hair was gathered in a bun, and a strip of fine down ran to the base of her neck. I was trying to capture her every detail. A few more hours and she'd be out of my life.

Zoll's driving grew more and more erratic. He must have been exasperated by my presence.

"Engaged," he suddenly exclaimed. "So does that mean you're going to get married?"

Now he was testing the determination of the future husband and wife. I opened my mouth to answer, but Emma beat me to it. She turned to me and searched for my hand.

"I've already introduced Antoine to my mother," she said, totally in earnest.

A sunbeam penetrated the car and lit up her face. There was something I hadn't noticed, and which the light suddenly revealed. There was a thin scar above her right eye, partly concealed by her eyebrow.

"Her mother's a fine cook," I insisted on pointing out. "A specialist in leg of lamb."

"Oh, leg of lamb," Zoll said greedily.

"It's all about the cooking time," I said.

It was a bit obvious, I know, but I was ready to say anything to make Emma smile. I was stocking up for the journey.

"I've also met her brother. A young man who practices all kinds of professions. Stuntman, knife thrower . . ."

"You never told me that!" Zoll exclaimed.

I wondered how long she'd keep holding my hand.

"Did you know her parents were circus performers?" I asked Zoll.

"No."

"Her mother was a famous tightrope walker."

"How interesting . . ."

Emma shook her head, the way you do with children who exaggerate. At that moment, the van slammed on the brakes, caught Zoll unawares, and we nearly hit it. Of course, instead of admitting that he was driving too close, the great man turned into a village lawman and, taking advantage of the traffic jam, got out of the car to yell at the driver through the van door.

"The family portrait came out really well," Emma declared.

"You think?"

In the end, our driver's impulsiveness suited me fine. It was good to be in the car together, just she and I.

"You can let go of my hand," I said.

She pulled away quickly, like a child caught red-handed.

"Do we have to play this comedy with the cast, as well?" I asked, worried.

"To be on the safe side. I don't know what kind of relationship the actors have with Zoll."

"Perhaps I'd better not say too much . . ."

"About what?

"About our relationship. I don't have your ease at playing a part."

She knew I was referring to the kiss, to the conviction she'd put into it.

"You're managing very well," she replied. "And thank you for taking it."

"What do you mean?"

"His coarseness," she said, indicating Zoll, who was getting all agitated outside.

"Oh, that, I don't care."

"Are you sorry?"

"About what?"

"About the detour."

"Not at all, but all good things must come to an end."

All of a sudden, she looked serious. I changed the subject.

"What's that scar above your right eye?"

"It's a long story."

"Too long to tell now?"

"Yes."

A concert of car horns started behind us. I got the feeling of a goodbye. Zoll would be back soon, and, once again, I felt that almost imperceptible dizziness. I put my hand on my forehead.

"Are you alright?" Emma asked, worried.

I pulled myself together.

"When we get there, you'll immediately go look for the company manager."

"You told me. I got it."

"I want to make sure."

3

The *Trois Soleils* company had taken residence in an old beret factory. The derelict building was between an abandoned basketball court and a bypass leading to a gigantic shopping center in the south of the city. No helicopters or caviar here, but a declaration of principles written on the front of the building—"Culture isn't inherited, it's conquered"—along with the name of the author, André Malraux. The M was quite damaged, though.

The actors were in the middle of rehearsing, and we slipped into the room without making too much noise.

"They're working on the scene when the tomb is opened," Zoll whispered.

A very handsome young man, dressed as a prince, emerged from the shadows and announced to the one who, seeing as he wore a crown, must have been the king, that Antigone was dead. Then he drew his sword and stabbed himself in the stomach without hesitation. Then a mature woman who was standing behind the king emitted a terrible scream and cut her throat before the frightened eyes of a blonde girl who looked very much like Cécile. After which the king was left alone on the stage, surrounded by corpses, and his only gesture was to straighten his coat.

"Perfect!" Zoll exclaimed.

The king stretched out his hand to help the woman, whose dress was covered in blood, get up, and she burst out laughing like a little girl.

"Good, I've finally nailed this scene!" she said.

Everyone congratulated one another while an assistant came with a pail and wiped away what was just dye. The rehearsal was over. Everybody immediately gathered at the bar, as though none of this bloodshed had taken place. They surrounded Emma and welcomed her by touching her and kissing her. There was a flow of comments, of laughter, and one of the actors, dressed as a guard, slipped behind the counter and started handing out coffees.

My cell vibrated. It was an SMS from Cécile. She was asking me to read my e-mails and signed off "with love," which puzzled me. Customarily, she would sign "kisses" and only used "with love" on special occasions. Besides, it was unusual for her to send an e-mail. She usually got impatient after three lines. She obviously had something important to tell me.

"Antoine!"

Emma gestured at me to approach so that she could introduce me to the company. The woman who'd just cut her own throat a minute ago opened her arms to hug me, and they all said hello to me in turn, as though I were a guest bestowing on them the honor of my presence. Then the group suddenly broke up. The woman who'd cut her throat took Emma under her wing and led her away to try on a costume, the giant stepped aside to make a phone call, and the king sat at a table, while Reinhart asked a young blonde woman to work with him on another scene.

"Want to keep me company?" the king said, behind me.

He'd removed his crown and his sandals. He rummaged through a plastic bag and placed on the table cured meats, cheese, bread, and even a bottle of wine.

"You see, I don't live at the same pace as these young people. I need a snack around now, but this evening, on the other hand, I'll just have some soup."

I sat opposite him. His name was Victor, and the authority

he oozed went far beyond his costume. He glanced at Reinhart, who was walking away with the young blonde woman.

"Ismene won't be enough for him. He wishes he could have Antigone. It would be a worthier trophy, though less accessible, since you're here. Would you like to try this pâté? I bought it at the Capitole market. What did you think of the scene?"

"I nearly rushed to help the prince, then the queen."

"You flatter."

"Not at all. Then that gesture you make with your coat . . ."

"Ah, so you saw it."

He handed me a small sandwich, and I devoured it. The hospital food had left me hungry.

"A little wine?"

"Yes, please."

We clinked glasses as he raised his.

"I've acted in movies, too, you know," Victor continued. "I still do sometimes, when they need a venerable old man. I've worked for that guy who's built studios."

"You've worked for Huge?"

"Yes."

Huge was his nickname. Obviously, nobody called him that to his face. He'd conquered audiences around the world with movies for children that grown-ups watched. Huge had offered Victor the part of a druid in an interstellar saga.

"Do you know him, too?"

"Yes, quite well," I replied.

"He looks so lonely. Everybody is, but I found it more widespread in the movie industry. And do you know Bourdet?"

"Not very well. He fired me too soon."

Gilles Bourdet was one of the champions of social realism movies, but for general audiences. He tackled powerful, current topics, migrants, people riddled with debts, and had a talent for surrounding himself with stars and giving a charming tone to his themes. However, he was very moody, to the point that he could speak to you as a friend one day and drag you through the mud the next, while at the same time advocating more justice and care for others in his films.

"Really? He fired me, too!" Victor exclaimed. "He accused me of not knowing my lines when, actually, he'd changed them the night before and didn't remember he did it. He drinks, doesn't he?"

"If that's what it is, he gets nasty after a few drinks."

We burst out laughing. We dropped other names, listed other follies, while enjoying his very delicate sheep's cheese.

While we were talking, the giant dressed as a guard came up to us. He looked annoyed. He'd spent all this time on the phone.

"What's the matter, my dear Boris?" Victor asked.

"Alibert won't be back till tomorrow."

"So?"

"So he was supposed to give me an advance. I promised the bank."

"How much do you need?"

I let them conduct their negotiations, and once we were alone again, I started asking Victor questions. I wasn't really worried, just on the alert.

"Is Alibert the company manager?"

"Yes, that's right. He's gone to Paris to collect some money."

"Is he likely to come back later than tomorrow morning?"

"Definitely not. We have to be ready to get to work tomorrow night, and he knows that better than anyone."

And now I really had to read my e-mails.

"Do you know if there's WiFi here?"

"I don't think so, but possibly at the hotel. It's on the other side of the bypass. Reinhart is the only one who doesn't sleep there. He's at the Mercure."

At that moment, Emma appeared, dressed in a long, ocher

dress. She was barefoot, without jewelry or finery, but she was glowing. You could tell from the expression on her face that the dress was a way of making the role her own, and that the process had begun.

"We've been getting to know each other," Victor said. "We have acquaintances in common . . ."

Emma sensed that I was on edge. She took me aside and took a close look at me.

"Are you alright?" she asked.

"The company manager won't be back till tomorrow."

"You'll have to spend one more evening with me, that's awful."

"You seem amused by the situation."

"That's not it. I'm sorry for this delay. But these people are interesting, you know . . ."

"That's not the point."

"Then what is the point, Antoine?"

She was staring at me. I felt like Creon undergoing Antigone's assault. There was nowhere to hide from those eyes.

"I must go to the hotel," I said. "I need to check my e-mails. Can I do that in your room?"

"Yes, of course. I think we'll be rehearsing until nine. Then we'll go and have dinner."

"Do I have to be there?"

"I'm afraid so."

"This dress suits you."

"Thank you."

4

The Royal Toulouse was easy to find, being the only hotel for a kilometer around. Who else would have wanted to fall asleep to the lullaby of the bypass, with a piece of waste ground in guise of a garden, except for more or less legal immigrants, backpackers put off by city center prices, or entertainers? The establishment must have recently changed hands since work was being done on every floor, and, frankly, it was nothing luxurious at that. Without a serious intervention, collapse was certain.

The reception area was covered in tarpaulin, and I carried on as far as the kitchen, where a man of African origin, probably a Fulani, given his height and elegance, was peeling potatoes. He stopped what he was doing to take me to Emma's room. It was right beneath the roof, and, as we climbed the stairs leading to it, he introduced himself. He was, indeed, of Fulani origin, and his name was Sonny, as a tribute to the famous Brazilian soccer player Sonny Anderson, of whom his father was a fervent admirer.

The room was tiny, and I had to edge my way along the bed in order to reach the simple shelf that acted as a desk.

"If you have any problems, you must talk to Ardashir," Sonny said before slipping away. "He's the owner."

I took my computer out of its case and switched it on, relieved to see that the electricity hadn't been cut, which was something. Then I struggled for a moment to get a connection and opened my inbox. I saw Cécile's name in the middle of the usual list of local sexual services, lucrative offers aimed at rich people, and ads for competitive loans. There were two messages from her. I opened the first one.

>Antoine,
>Given the circumstances, e-mailing seems like the best way to talk to you about this separation, which I think is necessary. I thought we could discuss this seriously before you left, and you must have sensed how incomprehensible I found your attitude. Since we didn't manage it, I told myself we would do it on your return, but you decided to delay that, and then I flew to Spain. Maybe it's best this way. It allows us to talk with a bit of distance.
>You're a charming guy, Antoine, and I have nothing in particular to reproach you with, but you're never there. At least you're not there with me. It's a feeling I got early on and which turned out to be true over time. Your mind is always somewhere else. Where? I ask myself that, but do you even know yourself? And then there was the DVD of Erik's movie which I really wanted you to see. Your lack of willingness to watch it illustrates how little importance you give to an opinion I may have about a work, and perhaps also the inconsistency with which you see your profession. I guess you had more important things to do with the people I alarmingly discovered during our Skype chat. I've never concealed from you the fact that I had ambition, Antoine, for myself as well as for you. You disregarded this chance I was offering you of, finally, a meaningful writing job and recognition, all for the sake of a game of tennis and an escapade of which I don't care to know the details. Success depends on talent, and you have it, that's something I've never doubted, but it equally requires willpower and the ability to make choices. Apparently, that's impossible for you.

She then went on to the "practicalities," as she called them—the apartment, to start with. She thought I'd agree to let her keep it, since she'd been the one who chose it and furnished it, and her life was in that district, which was true. The end of the paragraph sounded more ironic to me. Perhaps it concealed some bitterness. She claimed that my love of hotels would finally find an outlet, until I found something else, and I understood that she was asking me to pack my bags as soon as possible. Finally, she ended with some concern for me, which I felt was sincere.

> Don't take this the wrong way, Antoine, but by seeking the impossible, one often gets lost. Look after yourself.
> With love,
>
> Cécile

I opened the second e-mail. It wasn't addressed directly to me but was a collective e-mail Cécile had written to her female friends, and my address had been included, surely inadvertently. It was a kind of photo coverage of her stay in Marbella. Brendan Lamar's villa was built right by the sea, and its occupants had the choice between bathing on the private beach or floating on their backs in the infinity-edge swimming pool. Everything else was along the same lines.

Cécile must have taken these pictures with her phone, early in the morning, when her host was still asleep, in order not to seem like a tourist, because you couldn't see anyone in the frames, no matter which angle she used.

I clicked through the shots quickly; it was all more or less the same, as though she couldn't believe there was such luxury and that she'd been invited into it. Then I came across a series with the actors of this sunny sitcom: Lamar, the lord of the manor, and the famous Erik Arlo, whom I was seeing for the first time, the kind of guy who wears sunglasses in a nightclub.

All around them, heaps of pretty creatures genuinely happy to be there, at least as much as Cécile who, of course, had finally turned her device around so she could include herself in this landscape of winners.

I sat staring at the screen for a moment, then I closed my inbox and unplugged my computer.

Trying to be a little objective, I'd had it coming.

I quickly left the room. The first floor was quiet, and in the kitchen the back door was opened on the waste ground. There, Sonny was playing with two little girls, twins he was carrying on his shoulders and happily twirling around at full speed. A couple was watching them, almost certainly the owners of the hotel. The man, short and wiry, was drinking coffee, crouching, and his wife had one hand on his shoulder and was using the other as a visor to shield herself from the beams of the setting sun. I went up to them.

We said hello, and Ardashir, since that was his name, explained that he was Iranian and had been in Europe for twenty years. He'd opened his first establishment in Frankfurt but found the city rather sad, then made a foray over to the Côte d'Azur, hated it, and finally settled in the Southwest, where he liked the people, who were more open and cheerful.

I crouched down, too, so I could be at the same level as he while he was talking to me. He had incredibly piercing eyes.

"Do you have children?" he asked.

"No."

"How old are you?"

"Forty-one."

"Children are the salt of life, my friend."

I didn't have time to answer because his wife shot a volley of words at him.

"She says it's rude to ask a man if he has a family."

Sonny collapsed into the dust, and the twins covered him with kisses, preventing him from getting back up. Their mother spoke to them, like a whip cracking, and they let the valiant Fulani representative pick himself up. It was a happy family. I knew one when I saw one. As far as I was concerned, I wasn't ready to start one. The problem wasn't women, it was me. All the women I'd met had, sooner or later, became aware of my limitations. Cécile's e-mail was spot on. It's true that I was always "going along with" the other person, but I never went beyond that, I never built anything. She was right about everything, including the fact that my mind was elsewhere, though I couldn't say where exactly.

"Are you an actor?" Ardashir asked.

"No, my friend is."

All of a sudden, I realized I was going to spend the night with Emma in that tiny room. Great. That was all I needed right now.

"Don't you have to go back to her?" he asked.

"Excuse me?"

"Your friend. Don't you have to go see her?"

"Yes, of course."

On my way to the theater, I wondered if Emma would be able to guess that I'd just broken up with someone. I was already imagining the questions I'd have to face, if so, and cursed Alibert and his postponed return.

I reached the old factory and walked along the side wall. Raphaël was pacing up and down, phone glued to his ear, and waved at me.

When I came into the room, Emma was on the stage, facing Victor, or Creon, rather. She was confronting him.

"You all disgust me with your happiness! With that life you have to love no matter what! Like dogs licking anything they find. And that little bit of luck every day, if you're not too demanding. I want everything, all at once—in one piece—or else I refuse! I don't want to be modest, to be content with a small bit if I've been a good girl . . ."

I approached slowly, just to see her face closer. There was a stillness about her that made her powerful. I was about twenty meters away from the stage, and yet I felt I was being touched by her breath. Suddenly, she hesitated, as though stumbling, and I thought she'd forgotten her lines, but no, it was a motion of the character's spirit. She wanted to show us that it wasn't that easy for Antigone to resist, that she was on the edge of a precipice and that her feet were touching the abyss. The pause was exactly right. It was so generous of her to allow us to be closer to her through this minute wavering of her will.

Now she was back on the battlefield. And it was the king who was staggering. The twig was confronting an oak, but her rage was so contained, she was so articulate, that she commanded the respect of Creon himself.

"I want to be sure of everything, today, not tomorrow, and it must be beautiful. Like when I was a child. Yes, sir! We are the kind who ask questions to the very end! As long as there's just a tiny bit of hope left alive, we are the kind who leap on that hope of yours! We never leave it alone, that hope of yours!"

"Stop!" Zoll shouted, walking into the field of light.

He joined them on the stage, and, while he was talking to them, Emma cocked her head to one side and relaxed her arms, the way swimmers do on the starting block. All the tension of the confrontation had dropped. She was most definitely my opposite. I could still see it while she stood in the light and I in the shadow. I kept the world at an arm's length while she walked toward it, challenged it, ordered it to fight, no matter what the dangers or the number of enemies.

6

The entertainers were pleased with the way their day had gone, and they were hungry. Boris knew a restaurant in the old part of Toulouse that offered a single-course menu at a reasonable price. Zoll excused himself. He was having dinner with the city's culture officer, something he presented as a sacrifice although it was blatantly obvious that he got more out of that than hanging around with the foot soldiers.

We took a bus to the city center. Everybody sat at the back, and Raphaël began singing, "N'avoue jamais, jamais, jamais . . . ,"[3] and the others joined in. I don't know what André Malraux would have thought of it, but it was convincing enough.

The restaurant stood on the corner of a square where there was a statue representing a couple of lovers kissing. The place was friendly, looked like a barn, and was decorated in a whimsical style that bore witness to the rebellious spirit of the owner, a man called Silvio. Here, you could choose to play table soccer, watch rugby on the large screen, or sit in the dining room, furnished solely with three large farm tables and benches, which were shared by the various patrons.

That evening, the single course was lasagna, much to every-

[3] "Never, never, never confess . . ."

142 · ALAIN GILLOT

one's delight. Victor managed to negotiate some pesto soup, which was all he wanted. We took over the corner of a table, and the owner marked our territory with two jugs of wine he described as "honest," which meant it was quite strong. Emma sat opposite me and Émilie beside me. Boris and the owner had developed a kind of complicity, and he ordered some antipasti from a distance. Raphaël and Victor, then everybody else, took part in a summit, the purpose of which was to work out how to pay for this meal, which promised to be abundant, and that's when I gathered that at least three of them had nothing in their pockets and were relying on an advance the company manager had promised to give them, tomorrow, just before the tour started. However, that didn't cause any particular problems. It was like a ritual they practiced without a second thought. Those who were better off lent money to the others, that's all, and everything was sorted in a minute.

The lasagna arrived, piping hot, and Silvio took it upon himself to cut it into portions, saying he was keeping another dish of it warm for them. Émilie was glued to my arm. I hadn't noticed. It was Emma's expression, a touch ironical, that warned me. The beautiful Ismene had decided to take an interest in me, and there was a volley of questions. She wanted to know everything, about my job, my experiences, the company I kept, and wished me to draw her a precise and complete picture of the wonderful world of the silver screen, and point out, as I went along, the best way for her to get into it. No matter how hard I tried to tell her that there was no hard and fast rule about it, and that my experience was limited to my modest career—an argument I always kept in reserve to safeguard my tranquillity—it was no use. On her third glass of wine, she asked if I could introduce her to a casting director, I was bound to know some important ones, and, on her fourth, she talked of coming with me on a shoot, though she promised she'd be discreet and not get in the way of my work. Very considerate of her.

It was Raphaël who saved me by suggesting a mixed doubles game of table soccer. Emma immediately got up and asked me to be on her team, but I politely declined. I took the opportunity to check my messages. I hadn't heard my cell vibrate, and yet I'd received an SMS from Cécile, asking me to call her back as soon as I could. I felt the need to splash some cold water on my face, and, looking at myself in the bathroom mirror, I thought that as soon as I returned to Paris, I'd have to take a room in a hotel near the Marché Saint-Honoré until I found another apartment. I liked that area, which was also close to Paul's office.

When I returned to the room, the game of table soccer was in full swing, to the point where Boris was twisting his rods at every shot, then straightening them back out to a chorus of his opponents' laughter, before putting the ball back in play.

"Has Victor left?" I asked Béatrice.

"No, I think he's getting some fresh air."

She was knitting, just like Creon's wife does for the paupers of Thebes in the play, but, in real life, for her grandson. I went out of the restaurant and selected Cécile's name in my address book while I searched for Victor. In any case, he wasn't on the square, so he must have gone for a stroll along the neighbouring narrow streets.

"Antoine?" Cécile said.

"Yes."

"Did you read my e-mail?"

"Of course."

There was a moment of silence, and I sensed her unease. I decided to reassure her immediately.

"Everything you say is true, Cécile. And you made the right decision."

"Do you really think so?"

"Yes."

I felt her relax, out there in Marbella.

She had definitely left the house in order to take my call. You could hear the sound of a party in the distance.

"So you agree with everything, then?"

"It's always been your apartment."

"You know, I really appreciate this . . ."

"It's only natural."

She paused, then continued.

"There's something else I have to tell you. I don't want you to hear it from somebody else."

It was about Erik Arlo. She had taken the plunge with him, shortly before deciding to send me her e-mail; she didn't specify that, but it was obvious.

We spoke of various other things for a while, and I think she was glad that I was so calm. She had hoped we'd have that emotionally distant approach, but reality is sometimes different from intentions. She asked if I'd ended up watching the DVD, and I replied that I'd found it "extraordinary." I was playing with words, of course, but I wasn't lying. In a way, it was. Naturally, in this new context, it would be a problem for Erik and me to work together, and she hoped I would understand. On this point also I gave her what she wanted. I'd had a narrow escape.

I sensed she was hesitating to ask details about my "detour" to Bordeaux and my relationship with the people who'd appeared on her computer screen, but she finally opted not to. What did she stand to gain by it now? Nothing. Besides, the party behind her was in full swing.

We said goodbye and wished each other good luck. After I hung up, I stood there for a moment on the sidewalk, until I smelled a whiff of cigar smoke wafting through the air. I turned around. Victor was sitting on a stone bench, in the semi-darkness. I sat down next to him, facing the empty square, where all you could hear was laughter from inside Silvio's restaurant.

"What I've just witnessed was a breakup, right?" Victor said.

"Yes."

"You don't look upset by it."

"I guess not."

"Should I deduce that you're not engaged to Emma? Unless you lead a double life, that is."

"We have a deal. We're acting out this comedy until she signs her contract."

"So that she may be better protected from Zoll?"

"Exactly."

"That's very sensible. But there's something between you anyway, isn't there?"

"Between us?"

"Between you and Emma."

"Not at all."

Victor lit his cigar again. The ember turned red in the night.

"I didn't phrase it correctly. You have a connection. It's obvious."

"You mean like a father and daughter?"

Victor burst out laughing.

"I don't see what's funny," I said.

"You're dealing with the wrong person, my friend. Or rather the right one."

"I don't understand . . ."

"Well, as it happens, I married my drama teacher. I was eighteen and she forty-one. She was incredibly beautiful. All the students dreamed about her. They called her *the unattainable*. For two years, we resisted, meeting in cafés. We'd spend the whole night talking. We'd eat, drink, go to shows, everything was better when we were together. Then one day, I decided that we had to experience physical love. If it didn't work out, we could laugh about it. If it did, it would mean everlasting happiness. What did we have to lose by trying?"

"So what happened?"

"We did it, and we lived together for thirty-seven years without ever getting bored or feeling lonely. But it wasn't always easy. She found our age difference uncomfortable. She would say, 'So do you enjoy taking your mother out?' And she wasn't joking."

"What about you?"

"Did I have a problem with it?"

"Yes."

"Of course, I mean, sometimes. During the last years, she'd ask me to walk in front of her so that I couldn't see her struggling. But I never considered living without her. The only thing I resented her for was leaving before me. I'd hoped that an accident, an illness—not too painful, though—would upset the logic of time. I even considered suicide, but that seemed disloyal. In the end, she did me the courtesy of dying old, even though she never really seemed it."

"Was this a long time ago?"

"Twelve years. Might as well have been yesterday."

He fell silent. He was with her, in his recollections.

7

It was two o'clock in the morning, and the buses had gone back to the depot. Silvio ended up throwing us out, but as he was closing the shutters, he noticed Victor dragging his feet, so he lent us a bicycle. He'd have time to collect it from the hotel later.

As soon as we were outside, Emma took my arm. I felt I was getting used to it, it really was time for me to take a plane.

At that time of night, it was just us roaming the streets of the old town. Our footsteps echoed on the cobbles, our shadows spread along the fronts of the buildings, and you had to look high up to find anyone who was still awake. The night belonged to us. Raphaël was walking ahead. Boris was steering the bike, and Victor sat astride the carrier. Like us, Émilie and Béatrice were arm in arm, almost like mother and daughter.

"Émilie's stuck on you," Emma said teasingly.

"The Tarn wine has a lot to account for."

"The wine simply gave her the courage to speak out."

"You exaggerate. She'd just like to do some film work. I thought you were very good in your scene."

"You're changing the subject."

"Yes."

"Is she not to your taste?"

"I'm through with blondes. Victor was also brilliant. You understand everything he's saying even with his back turned."

"We're far from ready, you know. Come and see the play at the end of the tour, and you'll see the difference."

I didn't respond. If I managed to escape, it was essential that I didn't turn back. We were now in a narrower street, with loose cobblestones, and Victor was holding on to Boris to avoid being thrown off.

"What I find particularly surprising," I said, "is the impression you give that you've all known each other for ages."

"It's part and parcel of being in the theater. We're used to sharing. If you think only of yourself on stage, you're screwed."

"The fact that you're able to say your lines just like that, at the drop of a hat."

"It wouldn't have been the case for everything. As it happens, it's *Antigone* that made me want to be an actress. I passed my drama school exams with Sophocles's play. I played the Brecht one at the Amandiers Theater in Nanterre, but Anouilh's version is my favorite. His Creon is a reasonable man. That's his downfall. It's a very subtle take on the tyrant."

"Isn't reason a good thing?"

"It's not enough."

"Still, Creon survives."

"But he ends up alone. What's the point of ruling over a desert?"

I got the feeling she was talking about me. Wasn't that my story? The story of all men who go to such lengths to shield themselves from the world that they forget to factor in a door.

"Also, I love his Antigone," Emma continued. "Her complexity. When it comes down to it, all our choices are linked to our need for pride. It's what gives us the strength to accomplish great things, but it also blinds us. In high school, I had a philosophy teacher who'd set us the question: What are you proudest of? It was very revealing. What would your answer be?"

"Me?"

"Yes."

"No idea . . ."

"That's a cop-out."

"What about you?"

"I'll tell you if you play the game. Come on, make an effort."

I smiled. It's not that I didn't want to answer her, but I had to look back in time and find some tangible examples.

We crossed an intersection, and on the other side the road sloped down. Raphaël perched on the bicycle handlebars, and the three of them, Boris, Victor, and he, improvised a circus number.

"So?"

"I need to think about it."

We came to a square, quite small, framed by arcades, where our voices were amplified. The moon was full above the rooftops, and Raphaël couldn't resist.

"There you are, you livid face!" he began reciting, addressing the pale orb. "If Republicans were real men, what a revolution there would be in the city tomorrow!"

Emma whispered into my ear.

"It's from *Lorenzaccio*."

"Ah, words, words, eternal words!" Raphaël continued, on a roll. "If there is anyone up there, he must certainly be laughing at us all."

A light came on in the building opposite, and a large man appeared at the window.

"Now this, indeed, is comical," Raphaël went on, unperturbed.

"Shut the fuck up!" the man yelled.

"Oh, human chatter!" Raphaël persisted. "Oh, ruthless murderer of dead bodies!"

The large man disappeared for a moment, then came back to the window, and, before Raphaël could react, poured out the contents of his garbage can over him.

"Oh, man of little faith!" Boris exclaimed while Raphaël was shaking himself.

At the same time, we heard the sound of a siren. The man must have called the police, or else it was other residents who hadn't shown themselves. The performance was over, but Raphaël wanted his curtain call. He grabbed an envelope from the scattered garbage, which provided the address of his one and only audience member.

"Jean-René Plantier!" he said bravely. "3 Place des Aubiers, fifth floor, door on the left. Why dost thou turn away from me? I am but the humble herald of thy doubts!"

We had to drag him away from the square, the siren was drawing closer, and we penetrated a labyrinth of streets so narrow that they shielded our escape. Raphaël wheeled the bicycle, and Boris carried Victor on his back. We ran like bats out of hell until we were out of breath, then we stopped to rest. Since we could no longer hear the siren, we resumed our night roamers' pace, and, after walking alongside a park, we found ourselves by a pond in the middle of which rose a statue that supplied it with a constant stream of water. Raphaël immediately undressed. He went into the water in his underpants and, even though it wasn't very deep, started swimming.

"It feels good," he said.

Victor removed his shoes and socks and sat on the edge to have a foot bath. Émilie quickly followed his example, and soon everybody was playing with the water, except for Boris, who kept himself at a distance.

"He recently lost his mother," Emma said. "He arrived too late for them to talk, and that's tormenting him."

Our little company went on its way. Around here, the houses were much lower, and you could now hear the noise of the traffic that circled the city. We must have been quite close to the bypass.

Emma had found a way of holding my arm in such a way that even though our bodies were very close, they didn't get in each other's way. I often noticed that it was difficult for two people to walk in step with each other, I mean without forcing themselves. It was a question of height, hips, rhythm, a mysterious process that made it either ridiculous or pleasant. With Emma, I could have strolled like this all night.

"What happened with your parents, exactly?" she asked. "I mean, how did they die?"

"I didn't get there in time for my father," I replied, "but I was there for my mother."

I'd spent the last night with her in the detached house they had rented somewhere down south, once they had retired. My sisters were in the corridor, arguing over a ring, I think, and my father was slumped in his armchair. We didn't have time to talk, either, but that wasn't because of anybody arriving late, like in Boris's case, but because of something much deeper. Our entire relationship had been wordless. My mother had started to spit up blood, and I became a kind of intermediary between her death and the rest of the family. Then the doctor came to say that there was nothing more to be done, and I closed the door to find myself alone with this person about whom I knew nothing, even though I had come out of her womb. I put a chair next to her bed, listened to her breathing slow until it became just a rattle and then fell silent forever. And I stayed with her, holding her hand as she looked up at the ceiling, her mouth open, trying to give one last cry that would never leave her throat.

I swear, at that moment, I really wanted to cry, pour out all the tears my body possessed, abandon myself to my grief, but as usual, I couldn't, so I remained motionless, staring at my mother—this mystery—in the total silence of the room until daybreak. Then I opened the door and went to tell the others that it was all over, and as they rushed to the bed, I sat in the kitchen to have something to eat and a glass of wine, looking out at the garden, wondering what I was doing there.

"Hey, lovers, lagging behind?" Raphaël called back.

"Oh, enough, you," Emma replied.

I realized we were getting closer to the hotel, where the two of us would have to sleep in the same bed. I'd almost forgotten.

Could I tell Emma about this guy who never cried? Would she understand him? Of course she would. She was able to hear anything, the daughter of the hanged man and the lost madwoman, the sister of the knife thrower. She'd skipped several grades in the school of life. She was miles ahead of the Céciles and the Caroles of this world. It wasn't even a fair comparison. She frequented Sophocles and knew about the loneliness of kings, the sea currents, and every dance step. She had already seen so much and never closed her eyes. And that was it, that was what I was facing, the fact that she understood everything so quickly and so well. Up to now I had known only loneliness, which is a kind of adversity but which I had learned to live with quite well. With her, I was discovering a new kind of danger—sharing.

"You're far away," Emma said.

"What?"

"I said you're far away."

"Oh, not that far . . ."

The bypass appeared ahead of us, and as we walked underneath it, I looked up. It was like a new kind of cathedral, with God expressing himself through the quivering concrete. But it was only the trucks.

8

Ardashir was up when we reached the hotel. He suggested a drink to celebrate our imminent departure, but all anybody wanted to do was go back to their rooms, so in the end I was the only one left in the kitchen. It's not that I was desperate to get drunk, the evening had been boozy enough, but I saw this as an opportunity to let Emma go up to bed and fall asleep on her own before I went up, too.

"Try this, my friend," Ardashir said, filling a glass of vodka to the brim for me, and another one for himself.

"I thought Muslims didn't drink alcohol," I said mockingly.

"You're joking, I hope. Tehran nowadays is like Chicago during Prohibition."

Sonny came into the room, and Ardashir invited him to drink with us, just to annoy him. Sonny, who seemed to be getting ready for a nocturnal expedition, grumbled that we were heathens.

"This morning's the market, " Ardashir said. "I've offered him the van a hundred times, but he only trusts his feet."

"Is he going now?"

"He prefers to finish his night over there. To be woken up by the market gardeners as they set up."

Ardashir insisted I have one more drink, and as I walked up the stairs leading to the rooms, I realized it had been one too many.

Once upstairs, I hesitated to knock. I would wake Emma up if she was already asleep, so instead I decided to risk appearing rude and went in. The mattress had disappeared, and I wondered if I'd gotten the wrong room or if Sonny had given up on his repairs. I was about to go back down when Emma came up behind me, holding a candle.

"Come, I'll show you where we're sleeping," she said. "It really wasn't possible in this room."

She guided me along the corridors to a very steep staircase leading to a trap door that allowed access to the roof terrace.

"Boris helped me carry the mattress. The view is magnificent, you'll see."

It was true. You could make out the lights of Blagnac airport to the south, the loop of the Garonne to the west, and it was odd to think that I had jumped into that river barely forty-eight hours ago. Some days are fuller than others.

Emma had brought from the room everything you needed in order to sleep, at least on a summer night without storms. Sheets, pillows, a blanket, candles she had arranged on the edge of the roof, and a bottle of water in case we were thirsty. I made a desperate attempt to run away.

"Everybody's asleep, and Zoll isn't going to suddenly decide to do an inspection now. Don't you think we could sleep separately?"

She looked at me with a certain degree of pity.

"Alright, forget I said anything," I sighed.

She started to undress and, much to my relief, kept her underwear and T-shirt on. However, I could still see enough to remain on the alert. Then she sat cross-legged on the blanket, rummaged through her bag, and took out a small mother-of-pearl box.

"What's this?" I asked.

"I smoke before I go to sleep when I can. It calms me down."

I couldn't keep standing forever, so in the end I lay down on the mattress, as far from Emma as possible.

"You're going to sleep with your shoes and pants on?"

"I'll do as I please, O.K.?"

"I was saying it for you; after all, it's very hot."

She was right. The temperature had barely dropped, even though it was almost four o'clock in the morning.

"Oh, look . . ."

She pointed at Sonny, who was walking across the waste ground. He was carrying over his shoulder a stick from which bags were hanging. Soon, they would contain fruit and vegetables. His gait was a model of balance, his head high and arms like a pendulum, and he was singing softly.

"When you camp out along the River Niger," I said, "especially in Mali, one of the most beautiful things that can happen to you is to come across a group of Fulani who take advantage of the coolness of the night to travel. You can't see them, but you can hear them."

"You've traveled a lot."

"I used to run a TV travel program."

"Which were your favorite destinations?"

"Deserts. I feel at home in nothingness. Some people go crazy there, but for me it's the other way around, I feel peaceful in the desert. It's nothing to do with being an adventurer; actually, they're mostly a pain in the ass . . ."

"Who?"

"Adventurers. They know everything there is to know about suntan oil and brothels, they never let go of their pillows, and they always want the best spot in the tent. With them, it's like being at the office . . ."

"And which desert is the most beautiful, you think?"

"I haven't seen them all, but the Tassili n'Ajjer, on the Libyan border, is incredible. Blood-red sand and rocks that stand out like spaceships. Then there's the Ténéré, with its dunes tall as mountains but also as soft as silk. But what I was most impressed by is the salt desert in Bolivia. There's nothing like sleeping on a ridge of salt, at an altitude of four thousand meters. You feel as though you're on the deck of a boat sailing among the stars, and Earth is the boat."

"Didn't you want to stay there?"

"And do what? I couldn't imagine myself opening a travel agency or a bar. I don't have the nerve for tourism, and I distrust explorers, they always end up finding oil, and we all know what happens next."

She lit her joint. The smell of burning grass spread. I sensed that she was watching me, assessing me.

"What?"

"You betray your world with your tennis games and your Jaguar . . ."

"Not at all. I like sports. And cars. And lots of very ordinary things. I'm basically a softie unless somebody tries to get around me."

"You're not going to tell me you're happy in this society."

"Is this Antigone speaking or you?"

She laughed.

"Do you want to try this?"

"No, thanks."

"I think it's time you answered the question."

"Which question?"

"The one about pride."

"Don't you think it's a bit late?"

"We won't have time tomorrow, and I know perfectly well you won't come back."

One of the candles had gone out. I was so tense at that moment that I felt reassured by the fact that Emma was more or less validating the end of our escapade. This happens during a match, when you're neck and neck with your opponent, and, suddenly, your game plan seems clearer. You find your bearings in space and time and allow yourself to breathe. It doesn't mean you leave the game, but you're less worried about the outcome, you take it one point at a time, so you automatically play better.

"What are you thinking about now?"

"About tennis."

"I'm waiting for my answer."

"I know."

A candle had gone out, and now another. With less light, we enjoyed the view in front of us more. There were clouds drifting toward the Atlantic. A barge was letting itself be carried by the current.

"Not being fooled," I said.

"That's what you're proudest of?"

"Yes. I've given it a lot of thought, you know."

"And how did you reach this conclusion?"

"I thought of situations I've experienced over time, and it became obvious. My earliest memory is linked to not wanting to be fooled. I was five years old."

"Tell me about it."

I'd already ventured farther with her than I ever had with anyone.

"Go on . . ."

The last candle had gone out, and the wind had nothing to do with it. It had simply melted. Paul was the person with whom I'd had conversations that came closest to the one I was having now, but they were nothing like this. There wasn't this danger.

"I'll answer the question, too," she pointed out.

A plane was preparing to land at Blagnac. It was making a loop in order to face the wind. It's what swayed me. I pictured myself boarding. Even if I jumped into the void, I could always cling to that departure.

"I ran away," I said.

"That's quite common, if I may say so."

"Wait till you hear the whole story."

"You're right. I apologize."

The plane landed gently. A dog barked on the other side of the bypass.

"I was in the last year of kindergarten. Every day, my mother or one of my sisters would drop me off. They'd leave me in a room where the teacher came to pick up all the children in her class. We would sometimes wait five, ten minutes until she came to get us and, meanwhile, we were watched by a teaching assistant. That morning, I had a strange feeling. I can't remember the details, just an impression, so to speak, an impression that something was askew. As though everybody was pretending."

"Pretending what?"

"Pretending. That it was all an act and that I had no place in it."

"You thought that at the age of five?"

"I didn't phrase it like that. It was something I felt."

"O.K."

"I got up from the desk where I was waiting, walked to the door and went out without anyone stopping me. The supervisor must have been busy. And so I was out on the street."

"Didn't the school warn your parents?"

"Yes, but by that time I was far away, and more to the point, I'd hidden. I hadn't just run away from school. I didn't want to go back home, either."

"So where did you want to go?"

"I had no other goal but to hide. I took refuge under a railway bridge. It was a place where odd types hung around. I discovered that later. I was very lucky. A railroad worker found me, it had gotten dark ages earlier, and I was freezing. And that's where the story begins. Otherwise, as you say, it's just running away."

Emma lay down next to me. I felt her shoulder against mine.

"I'd gotten pneumonia, but the doctor who treated me overdid it with the antibiotics. I started getting hemorrhages, I got weaker by the minute. They sent me urgently to the sanatorium. This happened to many children, I'm not telling you the story of *Les Misérables* here. What's interesting, I think, is my perception of these events. I felt somewhat dehumanized at the sanatorium. I mean I felt I could only rely on myself and that I had to mistrust anything the grown-ups told me. That's what I remember, not going tobogganing or decorating a Christmas tree. I went back home a few months later. And I didn't recognize my parents. My mother told me that later."

"She must have panicked."

"Yes, a little."

"Did you really not remember them?"

"No. I saw these people sitting in the front of the car. My father with his cap, my mother with a scarf around her neck. They were talking, and I felt very far from them, as though they were strangers. They looked like cut-outs, and, even though I eventually recognized them, that feeling never left me."

I realized I'd lost track of time. No doubt it was because of the vodka, but it wasn't just that. I felt as though these stars would always glow above my head and Emma would be beside me forever. The same mysterious feeling I'd had on the wooden pontoon in Cap-Martin. When all was said and done, you really could slow down time. It wasn't just a mental construct. You could even share this fragment of eternity.

"And do you know the reason you ran away?"

"I told you, it was that feeling of absurdity in school. What were we doing there, with our little coats and our polished shoes? Where were we going like that?"

"There's more to it," Emma said.

"What?"

"Something must have happened to you before that. It must have. You don't see the world like that at the age of five. You say that's your earliest memory?"

"Yes."

"I'm sure there was something else."

"No, I assure you."

"But of course, otherwise it's impossible. Let me give you an example. My deal is being insubordinate, O.K.?"

"That's what you're most proud of?"

"Yes. And I know why. It's not just in my nature but also because of a situation. My father adored me when I was little, we had some wonderful moments, until I turned twelve. We went diving together; it was brilliant, we were so close. Then, all of a sudden, I grow up, get my period, and start going out with a boy."

"You were precocious."

"Yes. And that's when everything changes. My hero turns into a bastard. He hounds me, controls the length of my skirts, constantly listens to messages for me on the answering machine, follows me when I have a date, comes into my room without knocking. He rummages through my underwear and calls me a whore. He hits me."

"He did that?"

"Yes."

"The scar—was it him?"

"No. Well, yes. He trapped me at the top of the stairs. I thought he was going to kill me just because I was looking him in the eye. I think he was actually ashamed. So I said, 'Go on, kill me,' and he let me go. And at that point, I let myself fall down the stairs. I wanted to show him that I wasn't afraid of being hurt, that the fear of pain wouldn't stop me from standing up to him."

"The insubordinate one."

"Yes, that's how I became that, even though, trust me, I was lively, mischievous—but a good girl. Do you understand what I mean now?"

"I understand about you but not about myself. There are different backgrounds, different causes. You can't generalize."

We remained silent for a few minutes. Inhabited by all that had been said.

She shivered.

"You're cold."

"A little. I'm going to get under the blanket. You should, too."

I checked the time on my cell phone.

"What time is it?" she asked.

"Five."

"Time to go to sleep."

"That's rich coming from you . . ."

I got ready to sleep, distancing myself from her as much as I could.

"That was a good conversation, wasn't it?" she said.

"Yes. Although you made me do most of the talking."

She pulled up the blanket to just under her nose.

"Do you know the quotation from Goethe, 'It's by being yourself that you become the other person'?"

"You seem to read a lot."

"I dance, and I also swim. And I eat a lot."

"Yes, I noticed that. And sometimes you make your hours."

"If nobody stops me."

I let her win this set. She'd more than earned it. The dog kept barking but more sporadically.

"Just as well we'll be parting soon," I said. "I couldn't keep up with your pace."

She turned on her side. I could see her shoulder, the curve of her nape.

"Nobody will stop me from being alive," she said.

PART FOUR
AGUSTIN MENDIBURU

1

It was broad daylight by the time I woke up. I was still on the rooftop, but Emma wasn't next to me anymore. I was sure she'd fallen asleep before me, and I'd kept my eyes open, contemplating the carpet of stars and wondering how I would live beyond this conversation, and also if I was correct in believing that nothing noteworthy had happened before my notorious escape.

I put my hand on the crumpled sheet. That's where she had slept. I remembered the very beginning of our adventure. When I'd found her under a hazelnut tree at the highway station, after we'd left Menton. I'd been right to see her then as a character from Lewis Carroll. There really was a door concealed in the bark of the tree against which she stood, and which, if you weren't careful, could lure you into a dizzying abyss.

That night, even though our skins hadn't touched for a second, or barely, I had gone inside her and she inside me, as deep as it was possible for us to go.

I sat up abruptly. Was I crazy to be thinking such things? Had the vodka eaten away at my brain or what? And what time was it anyway? Judging from the traffic, it wasn't very early. I checked the time on my cell phone. Nine-twenty already! I had to get a move on if I wanted to catch the noon flight after dropping by the theater. Because I had to go there, stage a successful exit, persuade Zoll to stay in his place, let the prospect of my return linger.

I hurtled down the stairs, preparing an excuse about the bed on the rooftop, but met Sonny halfway down as he was going up to clear everything away. Emma had already been to see him.

Since the kitchen was deserted, I went to reception to see if Ardashir was there and came face-to-face with Nahid, his wife. She started shouting at me as soon as she saw me, almost as loudly as when she addressed her husband, so I concluded that she had accepted me. The twins then appeared and clung to my pant legs. They gave me presents as though I were a family friend: a jacket button and a safety pin. I kissed their cheeks as hard as I could and thought that if I had children in another life, I'd like them to be twins and just as comfortably themselves.

I found a taxi almost right away, a novice who must have gotten lost in the area. I threw my bag in the trunk and, as my driver headed for the theater, read the first pages of the *Casablanca* remake. I think I wanted to turn it into a shield.

The screenplay was very well written and had a lot of "white space." One day, an Irish colleague who wrote the wonderful *My Left Foot*, which provided Daniel Day Lewis with one of his best roles, had given me the codes for Hollywood screenwriting. "They want a lot of white space on the page," he'd proclaimed. What he meant was that when working with Americans, you had to remain factual, minimalistic, as far as both stage directions and dialogue were concerned.

I got engrossed in a scene I found particularly well constructed, between Rick Blaine and the bar pianist, who played something of a medium in the story, and lost track of what was going on around me.

"This place has been shut down," the driver grumbled.

I looked up and got a shock. Seals had been put on the doors of the theater. I pretended I already knew, as I didn't feel like pouring my heart out to the taxi driver, so, sensing he was going to complain about how short the ride was—I just knew he would—I let him keep the change.

There was a sign next to the seals, saying that the place had been closed down by the District Court until further notice. Where were they all? I was about to go to the café on the other side of the bypass, thinking I'd find them there, when I heard a loud noise coming from inside. I looked through the keyhole. It was too dark for me to make anything out, but I became aware of a kerfuffle on the other side of the stage and decided to walk around to the other side of the building. Raphaël was sitting astride an upstairs window. It was easy to work out how he'd gotten there. They'd put a ladder on the roof of an old company minibus, a ladder I thought looked very much like the one standing in the hotel lobby, which meant that Ardashir must have had a hand in the conspiracy.

From atop his perch, Raphaël was throwing down the costumes, and Boris was catching them in his large arms, while Béatrice was stacking them up in the vehicle. Neither Émilie nor Emma could be seen anywhere, so I figured they must be inside trying to gather anything that seemed useful.

Slap bang in the middle of the empty lot, Victor was sitting in Creon's armchair, which constituted a piece of the loot. He was supervising the operation. He made a sign for me to join him, looking truly like a king granting an audience. He was smoking one of the cigars he saved for the evening, which meant he must have been somewhat nervous.

"Believe it or not, I am now the producer of this tour," he announced.

"Isn't the company manager coming back?"

"I'm afraid not. He was arrested at dawn in a hotel on Rue de Liège, in Paris. He was about to take a train to Belgium with the subsidy money. And that's not all. He's been embezzling cultural funds for years, it seems, and paying some of it back to those who've granted them to him."

"And you decided to carry on with the tour despite all this?"

"The dates are booked. It would be a shame to cancel. We've finished rehearsing, and none of us has a better solution. All we need is something to pay the operating costs with, at least for the first few days."

"And you're the one who's assuming the risk."

"I have a little money put aside, you know, I've had my moments of glory, and I won't be hurting anybody. Remember, I have no children, and Simone would have approved. Besides, it's not impossible we'll have a success on our hands, and in that case I'll make my money back."

He was sitting there, on his throne, wearing the clothes he was comfortable in outside work, shapeless tracksuit bottoms with holes at the knees, pantlegs tucked into his socks, open-work sandals. He was magnificent.

"Isn't what they're doing illegal?"

"Let's call it compensation against severe damages. A judge would grant us that. But since we were supposed to leave this morning, we couldn't linger on these details."

"What about the minibus?"

"Alibert had left the keys and documents, and even filled it up. He must have really not expected to be arrested. It's only once he got to Paris that he decided to run away, after he found out that one of his generous donors was being questioned."

"I don't see Zoll."

"Alas, he left us," Victor said with detachment. "I guess it was all a little too much for him, what with no more salary, no more Hôtel Mercure, and Antigone resisting him. Béatrice is going to replace him. She has directing experience, and her knitting can wait."

At that moment, there was a loud noise behind us. A spotlight had slipped out of Raphaël's hands and crashed onto the roof of the minibus, but nobody got upset. It was all part and parcel of the job.

Emma appeared at the window. She waved at me, and I responded. They also lowered a portico that acted as the cave where Antigone is walled up alive. It had to be taken apart before it could be lifted onto the vehicle's rack.

They completed their break-in, and Raphaël stood up on the top of the ladder.

"To leave!" he declaimed. "While my heart is amazed, to cut through the curtain of the unknown! Hear me, oh change-able fate! Open your arms to the intrep—"

The ladder swayed, and he clung to the window as best he could.

"Stop being an ass, please!" Boris shouted.

Finally, Raphaël came back down without accidents, followed by Emma and Émilie, and after Boris had checked the oil level, they were ready to set off.

"You're leaving too, aren't you?" Victor asked.

"Yes, I'm catching a flight for Paris at noon."

Emma came up to me. She must have explored the attic from top to bottom and clearly enjoyed the adventure. Her eyes were sparkling.

"You see, it takes more than that to stop us," she said.

"I never doubted it."

"We could drop him off at the airport," Victor suggested.

"That's very kind, but it's out of your way."

Emma was standing in the light. She squinted.

"That's not always a bad thing," she commented.

Everybody got into the minibus, with Boris at the wheel. He seemed to be an expert at group transportation. There was room for three in the front, and Emma sat next to me.

As soon as the vehicle started, Raphaël started hurling abuse. Sparing me was out of the question, so I was treated to the entire popular repertory on the theme of romantic farewells. Hervé Vilar, Joe Dassin, Dalida, Michèle Torr, François Valéry, experts only, all summoned. Raphaël's knowledge didn't stop at classical authors. Far from it. "A song, like a fareweeeellll, a dance for those in loooove . . ." A real massacre.

Emma leaned toward me.

"I've heard from my brother," she whispered. "He said the first few days were really tough, but he's beginning to feel better. He's left his room and enrolled in a workshop, and he's also met a girl he quite likes."

"And your mother?"

"She cut her hand opening oysters, but other than that she's fine. It turns out you really do like my family."

"That makes a change for me. Everything was very quiet in mine."

"And we're entertainment for you, is that it?"

"There's something in your hair . . ."

It was true. The attic must have been full of dust, cobwebs, and straw, and strands had gotten stuck in her hair. She tried to remove them but couldn't.

"I can do that, if you like."

"Alright, but be gentle, I hate my hair being pulled."

I did my best. I was very close to her. I could see her eyelids flicker. The small marks on her skin. The others started singing saccharine-sweet laments. I couldn't wait to get out of there.

Boris stopped outside the airport main entrance, I said goodbye to everybody and got off the minibus. Emma followed me.

"I wanted to thank you," she said.

"What for? After all that, you won't make your hours."

"Yes, but you tried very hard. That counts for something."

"True," I agreed. "I almost drowned, was attacked by an oven, did car acrobatics, and spent a night on a rooftop, risking pneumonia."

"As a sanatorium veteran, it'd be silly to have a relapse. I'd like to kiss you."

I was holding my bag in front of me. If I put it down, I'd be screwed.

"I don't see why you need to do that. Zoll's gone. The contract man is in jail, and you know Victor's worked it out. And I don't think the others fell for it, either."

"I'm not asking for their sakes, I'm asking for mine."

"Are you collecting? Doing a study? You like old men?"

I was defending myself as best I could. She shook her head, sorry for me.

"You idiot. Do you really think I get into a car with just anybody?"

"Well, I did get the impression you like to act mysterious."

"That's right. Actors. Are you going to kiss me, yes or no?"

They suddenly stopped singing on the minibus, as though they knew it was a difficult moment for me. I'd run out of arguments, and on top of everything else, we were holding up traffic, so I had to make a decision.

"Hurry up, then. You know I'm not into emotions."

"You're never taken in."

"That's right."

She did it. She kissed me. The insubordinate was capable of such tenderness.

The sun had gone, there was nothing anymore, it was like one of those deserts where I felt at home, all that was left was essentials, the salt of the earth, and even though I knew perfectly well what Ardashir meant, there weren't just children in life, there were also grown-ups, when they were still children.

2

The plane seemed to have been chartered just for me. It was originally meant to pick up a hundred and twenty-seven French tourists coming back after a cruise on the Nile and transiting through Blagnac before reaching their final destination, Roissy Charles-de-Gaulle. However, the Egyptian authorities had held their Airbus at Cairo airport because of a suspected bomb concealed on board, so I had no trouble finding a space in this great emptiness, even though I'd gotten my act together at the last minute.

I don't know whether it was because my presence significantly improved passenger numbers on the flight, but as soon as I arrived at the airline counter, I felt as though I was being treated like a prince and that everything was being done to make my life easier. Thinking about it, that was probably just in contrast with the events of the past few days. In a way, I was returning to civilization. Here, nobody seemed to want to drown me, wreck my car, or make me swallow a piece of charcoaled lamb. It seemed I was entitled to the maximum luxury available to Western man, tranquillity, garnished with a clear goal that couldn't be upset by any dramatic turn of events, all made possible by my boarding pass. Funny, I thought I'd have to run to make this flight, and now I was early, with at least two hours to kill. There was no question, though, of leaving all this free time unfilled and risking my mind wandering. Even though it bore the signature of a farewell—which is why she'd indulged in that extravagance—Emma's kiss was still too present in my mind for me to lower my guard. And the best way to protect myself during this delicate moment before my departure was to get back to basics, work, followed by some relaxation as a reward.

I sat at the most remote table in the food court and planned the two hours to come. The first would be devoted to Paul, about time, too, and to this *Casablanca* remake project. The second to a detailed reading of *L'Équipe*, from which I expected neither surprise nor deep emotions but simply a little distraction.

What I remembered of Curtiz's multi-award-winning movie was that it was a story of departure. I had in my mind the picture of Bogart leaving Bergman next to a plane with already spinning propellers, and I recalled quite a heartrending goodbye, a kind of sacrifice. The airport WiFi was quite effective considering it was only a temporary contract of one euro fifty, and it was easy to find a summary of the film. In actual fact, it's a refugee story. While the German occupation is ravaging Europe, the hero, portrayed by Bogart, a certain Rick Blaine, moves to Casablanca after a heartbreak. Prior to this, he is madly in love with a young woman who vanishes overnight without an explanation. He is now the owner of a bar in the "White City" that accepts Germans, French, and Americans equally, a place of transit where all the various intrigues are played out before the disenchanted eyes of the owner, whose motto is "I stick my neck out for nobody." He couldn't be clearer. Except that one fine day, the young woman with whom he had the passionate affair in Paris arrives, with her husband. At this moment, things come to a head, and during the events that follow, Bogart finds out why Bergman had to join her husband, a leader of the Czech Resistance, whom she had thought dead—and also that she still loves him, Bogart. The movie then takes on its whole adventurous and moral dimension because, after parting with the lady, Bogart helps her husband, who is in a terrible jam, escape the Germans and pushes the couple onto a plane, having had his own faith in life restored and wanting to join the Resistance with a Frenchman called Louis Renault. The name made me smile in passing: if I did sign to do a treatment, I would make a joke by calling the American Cadillac.

I hadn't had anything to eat since I'd woken up, and I managed to find a slice of acceptable cake which I complemented with an American coffee. I tackled the second phase of my research. David Pachett's screenplay. I usually needed just a couple of hours to read a hundred-page script, but I could do it faster if I didn't take notes. Pachett set the story just after World War II, in a Berlin occupied by the Allies and the Russians, in the middle of the Cold War. It was a good idea. Rick's bar was in West Berlin, there was still the atmosphere of secret transactions and passport trafficking that was the basis of the original movie. However, I got a shock reading the ending, especially since Pachett was supposed to be the kind of author Paul represented, besides me, someone brilliant and with integrity. And here he was, suggesting an epilogue that quite happily betrayed the form and spirit of Curtiz's film. Bogart, in this case DiCaprio, boards the famous plane, its propellers now jet engines, on the arm of a Scarlett Johansson still in shock after her husband is shot dead in a cowardly attack by the Russians, and yet not in the least unhappy about finding her Leo again.

Is that why the script had been sent back for rewrites? I doubted it. I even thought this ending, devoted to the star system, was the reason why this circulating version was considered "nearly the right one," as a way of showing us, wretched Europeans who'd never gotten it, how to develop an audience's loyalty. I imagined they were already picturing a prequel. DiCaprio Rick, spearhead of the French Resistance, meeting his

Johansson in Vercors and fighting the nasty Germans, all called Volkswagen.

I finished my coffee and saw I'd received an SMS from Paul. He was asking me when I'd be back, because a member of the Paramount Pictures' management was in Paris, and he claimed he could arrange breakfast with him at the Meurice, in case I already had any ideas in mind. I couldn't give him satisfaction on this point but confirmed that I'd be in Paris early afternoon. I saw from his quick reply that he was relieved to find me safe and sound, even though at some point he must have doubted it.

I'd done enough work to have earned a break. In any case, I never found the solutions to a screenplay problem by staying stuck to a blank page or a screen. I wasn't that kind of a student. I needed a diversion, to unwind, with a game, a nap, so that my ideas would start to flow. The Paris flight would be perfect for that. I had a difficult moment, just as I left the food court. I know it's stupid, but I should have expected it and been more vigilant. Without thinking anything of it, I went up to the glass front to look at the planes maneuvering on the tarmac. A small Airbus was about to take off, and the airport staff were guiding it between the lines toward the runway. Planes still made me dream, like many people, I think, even though flying is now commonplace, and I went from dreaming to daydreaming. I suddenly saw Emma on the rooftop of the hotel, smoking, talking, then falling asleep beneath the stars while expressing her desire to be alive. A blast of heat swept over me, but I pulled myself together again very quickly. I had to hold on for just one more hour.

I bought *L'Équipe,* went to the departure lounge, and sat as close to my gate as I could. The benches were mostly empty, and I imagined the same place colonized by a battalion of tourists in Bermuda shorts coming back from a campaign in Egypt. I was lucky.

I sat away from the few people there: a couple, a woman of around fifty on her own, and a younger one with a child who must have been about the same age as Ardashir's twins. From where I was sitting I could see the clock, the images from a 24/7 news channel, and the boarding counter. I spread out my newspaper and started looking through it, but I was surprised to notice that I was struggling to take an interest in its contents. Nothing to worry about, I attributed this lack of enthusiasm to my tiredness, which was perfectly understandable after these eventful nights and the fact that I had hardly slept at all the night before.

The woman on the bench opposite me seemed nervous. She kept tugging at her son's clothes under the pretext of fixing them, as though walking through the gate was a fashion parade. At some point she practically tore off his cap and put it behind her to comb his hair.

I carried on turning the pages, looking for a topic likely to interest me. Djokovic had won the US Open, but in the margins of this rather too-predictable triumph, you could read an interview with Tony Nadal, Rafael's uncle, whose opinion counted for a lot in the field. The journalist had gone to see him in his Manacor den, and I paused on a paragraph in which he expressed all the positive things he thought of Amélie Mauresmo, the French champion who'd become Andy Murray's coach. Tony had no hesitation in attributing the Scottish player's success to her, stating that her female nature had led him to free up his game, just as Amélie's owning her homosexuality had helped her free herself from other people's opinions. He'd become more himself on the court, as you could see in the tie-breaks he now negotiated with much more confidence. I sat thinking about these remarks and felt the need not to go any further into the subject. It led straight to the necessity of meeting beings who push you to look at the world differently in order to evolve, and that wasn't a topic I particularly wanted to tackle at the moment.

That's when the child burst into tears. His mother had just given him a phenomenal slap, and I didn't have to strain my ears to understand that she was facing a major catastrophe—the kid had lost his cap. It had slipped under the bench, I could see perfectly well where it was, and I considered telling the mother, but as a rule I never minded other people's business, especially when they seemed rather hysterical.

I tried to find another article that would interest me and to forget about this cap business, but it was impossible. The mother was calling to witness the few other passengers present in the lounge. She was shaking her son, accusing him of all evils, in particular of forcing her to spend vast amounts of money on dressing him decently.

"Decent." Why had she used that word? Nobody did these days, but for me, it would forever be my mother's favorite adjective. She applied it to everything. To dress length, to the way one cleaned one's teeth, behaved at the table or in a shop, counted money, and even sex, on the rare occasion she'd let a comment slip on the subject.

Again I felt a little restless, but I forced myself to put things into perspective. Soon we'd be boarding, and I could even ask for a secluded seat, even if that meant paying a supplement. Besides, the stewardesses were approaching the counter, and I thought I was nearing my goal when the woman shouted at her son again.

Life's silly, sometimes. You delete a role in a screenplay, end up at Menton Station, facing a stranger at odds with the limitations of the regional train network, drive across France, run off the road, and from that moment on everything in your life is topsy-turvy. You're no longer in control of anything, and everything becomes possible, even getting up because of an issue that doesn't concern you when it would be much simpler to keep your seat.

"Excuse me, madame," I said.

I stood rooted in front of the woman, who was looking at me with the eyes of a stone marten surprised in her burrow.

"Excuse me, but the cap you're looking for is down there . . ."

"What?"

"The cap. It's there," I pointed at it.

The woman paused, long enough to assess my true intention. Was it to make fun of her, judge her, help her? This last option didn't seem likely, but to start, she opted to justify herself.

"He gives me such a hard time, you know," she said in an exasperated tone.

I hastened to assure her of my support. She'd made a mistake, but then who didn't? No need to overdo it. And as she quickly picked up the object of the dispute, I went back to my seat. I was not going to join the Resistance with Louis Renault, either. But then the shouts grew louder, and I couldn't stop myself from turning around.

"I'm warning you, next time . . ." she yelled. "You hear me? Next time . . ."

Finding the cap hadn't calmed her down, on the contrary, and I couldn't help but feel partly responsible for this escalation. Stupid, I know, but it's what made me turn back.

"Excuse me, madame," I said standing before her again. "Actually, you were the one who dropped it, the cap . . ."

This time, the surprise, the complaining were over. She was the object of a full frontal attack, as far as she was concerned, and no way was she going to put up with that.

"Why don't you mind your own business?" she replied in a markedly more aggressive tone.

She was what they call nowadays upper-middle-class. She

had a raw silk top and probably bank investments, but during conflict she was coarse. Funny—considering where I came from, we had something in common. It had taken me years to become civilized, while she could drop her standards within three seconds.

"You put it on the back of the chair, and it fell," I insisted, aware that I was getting entangled. "It's no big deal, I just wanted to—"

"What do you want, you jerk? You have children? Do you know what it's like? And you're giving me shit? In my life—"

I'd gotten what I'd deserved. I'd provoked her, and in front of her child to boot. What else could I expect from her?

"I'm sorry," I said. "I didn't want to—"

She lashed out. "Yeah, well, mind your own business."

I must admit, the walk back to my seat felt quite long. I was afraid of more shouting, but no, it was over, and when I sat down it looked like she'd forgotten about me or, even better, that the incident had never taken place. And this was true for all the people in the lounge. Why was I so surprised? It was in the order of things.

I folded my newspaper carefully, checked my ticket and my seat number. All I had to do now was wait for boarding to be announced, but I went and made another mistake. Sometimes, one is the consequence of the other, and you can't stop anymore.

And yet it was almost nothing, and in other circumstances it wouldn't have mattered, I simply raised my head and looked at the waiting area, its occupants, the plasma TV screen on which rows of refugees paraded between two insurance commercials, the clock, and me, in the middle of all this, on my bench. It was what they call in my field an establishing shot. What an idiot. The second I understood the danger, it was already too late, obviously. Too late to turn back, too late to close my eyes or find a riveting article about hockey. I was five years old, it was November in the kindergarten playground, and the trap closed in on me.

It wasn't because of the cap that I'd gotten up, and if it was for the child, it was rather for the one I had been than the one sitting there, who'd probably already moved on, at least I hoped so for his sake. No, if I'd gotten up it was in order to assess the influence I could have on the ongoing process. *The human journey.* To assess if I could walk into the picture and alter it. And what I had just discovered was that it was impossible.

It was the same old song. "Put your scarf on, tie your shoelaces, show me your fingernails." The bringing to heel began very early and never really stopped. The airport benches had replaced the school desks, stewardesses the teachers, but it was the same old tune. You punched your ticket but for an everlasting return trip, the tourist brochure sold pleasure, but necessity ruled no matter where you landed. You had to force yourself to be "decent," in my mother's words, and "a winner" in Cécile's. What was the difference? There was none.

The smooth voice of a stewardess was heard somewhere near the ceiling, inviting us to start boarding. The passengers stood up, and I decided to let them go ahead. The line would be short, and there was no point in standing around; besides, I needed some space. Ideally, at this very minute, I would be in a desert, except that I didn't have one to hand.

Finally, I got up, and that's when I felt really scared. It wasn't one of those small dizzy spells where you just wait for it to go. I lost my balance to the point where I thought I was going to fall. I was sweating, shaking. What was happening to me? I decided to look at something solid. Over there, beyond the stewardesses, the passengers were entering the jet bridge leading aboard the plane. I wanted to join them, I had to join them. Once I was in that passageway, everything would be alright. I took a step in that direction, but the ground disappeared from

THE BEST THING · 181

under my feet. After all, I knew I had to avoid public transportation. I undid the button on my shirt collar, desperately
searching for air. I was suffocating. It was painful. I wasn't
going to pass out now, was I? I had to get out.

I walked straight ahead in the midday light. I wasn't aware of everything. I knew I was crossing the access road to the airport, but I couldn't quite estimate its width or the speed of the vehicles that were cutting me off in every direction. A sedan drove past right next to me. I saw its driver threaten me with a fist, then a biker honk his horn like a madman while zig-zagging to avoid me. Luckily, a truck slowed down to let me through, and the other vehicles piled up behind it. I was able to get to the other side of the road.

I went into the parking lot and felt relatively safe between the rows of cars. I could lean against the bodywork whenever I staggered, and avoid people's looks. As I passed a van, a dog that was shut inside started barking, and I got the shock of my life.

There was work in progress at the end of the parking lot. A deep groove of at least two meters opened before me, and I took refuge in this gravelly shelter. It was like finding a tiny particle of beneficial nothingness in Blagnac, and I started to feel a little better. My breathing became regular again, and only the speed of my heartbeat still bore witness to the panic that had overwhelmed me. My thoughts fell slowly back into place. A goal was slowly emerging. Rent a car, find Emma, talk to her.

The day prior to their departure, before they knew that the manager of the Trois Soleils was a crook, Boris had shown me the stages of their tour on a map. It basically went through villages in the Basque Country, and I remembered the first name, which was quite musical to the ear: Esterençuby. Boris had sung the praises of the beauty of this valley, the gate to the Iraty plateau, and I knew roughly how to get there from Toulouse by taking the highway as far as Pau, then reaching Saint-Jean-Pied-de-Port by national road.

I also knew what I wanted to say to Emma. Paradoxically, even though I was still physically exhausted, I had quite a clear view of the situation. I couldn't spend my life running away, I had to discover what had once driven me in the first place and still did now. What I thought was a detour was now my principal itinerary, and, at the end of this road, there was a chance for me to find out who I really was, that is, if Emma agreed to help me. She was so strong, so insightful.

However, I had to be very clear with her and with myself. If I went back, it wouldn't be because of a kiss or any possible romance we'd hinted at in the past few days. We had to be lucid enough to rule out this romantic possibility that would lead us to a dead end. Our meeting was a true opportunity. I'd had my reservations at first, but now I was convinced. Moreover, it would only be an opportunity if we were able to experience together not the confusion of passion but this feeling I had discovered with her, which I'd never known before, of trusting someone to the point of telling them everything.

"Monsieur!"

I jumped. A mountain of a man was calling me from the edge of the embankment, just above me. He was wearing a suit that was slightly too tight on him and dark glasses.

"Please don't stand there, monsieur."

He was holding a walkie-talkie that was constantly emitting fragments of conversation.

"Come toward me, please."

He was polite the way you are with crazy people before putting a straitjacket on them.

"Give me your hand, monsieur."

He came down the slope a little and reached out his arm so that I could grab hold of it.

"Do you have a travel bag?"

"I felt faint . . ."

He looked me over, my shoes, my pants, my shirt, searching for a clue.

"We found an unlabeled travel bag in the departure lounge."

I put my hand on my forehead. I was still a little weak.

"Yes, that's right, I left it there. With my small bag."

"They destroyed everything."

"Excuse me?"

"It's the rule, monsieur. Security had to step in."

"Oh . . ."

This trip was truly incredible. I had first lost my car, then my girlfriend, and now my tennis rackets and work tool. I was undeniably heading toward a form of stripping down.

The security agent took me to the police office, and I found myself in a little grey room where I told the truth—it's sometimes simpler—to the civil servant taking my statement, that I'd been the victim of an overwhelming anxiety attack. The man had no trouble believing me. He told me his sister-in-law couldn't stand being in a movie theater because as soon as the lights went out she thought she saw skulls all around her. We were joined by the airport head of security. He was quite a short, lean man, a former member of the special tactical force GIGN. He apologized about my bag, explaining the current situation, and I said I understood completely.

He offered to take me to the car rental place and, on the way, told me he'd asked to be transferred to the Southwest to enjoy life a little after years of stress. He'd taken part in the bloody assault on the social services branch of the Garenne, an event the movies had grabbed hold of. He'd met with the screenwriters to tell them his version of the facts but then not heard anything from them, and he'd been a little hurt. I explained that it was very common in TV and radio to forget the sources used, and that he certainly shouldn't be offended. This practice was due to a concern not to increase the number of rights holders, as well as rudeness.

There was a wedding fair in town and the Europcar parking lot was practically empty. Still, I managed to find what I was looking for, a large car, in this instance a Volkswagen Passat, because I'd noticed that the minibus was bursting at the seams and figured an extra vehicle would not be amiss.

When I pushed the key into the ignition, I had a sense of true satisfaction. I had my independence again. If I drove fast enough, I could reach the company by mid-afternoon.

I stopped to buy a sandwich and sent Paul an SMS. I apologized for leaving him in the lurch and said an explanation would follow. It occurred to me that, now that Cécile and I had broken up, I didn't have anybody else besides him to inform of my movements. He was my last link to any form of social life, and if that snapped I'd have no more connections.

I resumed my cruising speed. The side wind was quite strong, and the trucks were swaying. I'd told Emma that my sisters and I had drifted apart "naturally," but things were less straightforward than I'd cared to specify. The real split took place when my father died. We couldn't manage to get together, even for a simple meal or a wake, in order to talk and decide things together, and that merely confirmed our inability to be a family. It wasn't anybody's fault. We hadn't been one during our childhood nor at the start of our adult lives, so why should anything change because of a bereavement? I'd distanced myself without resenting anyone, at least no more than myself. We had, each of us, led solitary lives in that house, never sharing our dreams or our laughter, or very little and only when brought together for obligatory rituals and unavoidable moments throughout the day, but then what was there to share? Like everybody else, we opened presents, but once the ribbons had been undone, the wrapping paper crumpled, and the fairy lights turned off, what was left? Nothing. Just like my parents, together and separately, my sisters remained a riddle to me, and I to them. Only once did I contact one of them. At first it all went well, until we broached the subject of our parents, our childhood, and then I realized that I would only hurt her. She wanted to keep happy memories of those years, fine, it was her right, but I could not compromise to that point. We hadn't seen the same thing, we were so different, so why force the issue? I gave up telling her anything, and, actually, I was relieved. I hope she was, too.

My cell phone vibrated.

"Hi, Paul."

I was glad he called. I'd sent that SMS in haste and wasn't happy with it, it wasn't like us.

"Are you alright?" he asked.

"I'm driving toward the mountains."

"Is it still that young woman?"

"Yes. Well, it's more about me, but I need her in order to see things more clearly. Are you very angry with me?"

"Why?"

"Because of that guy from Paramount."

"Oh, him . . . He'll wait. That's not why I'm calling. It's about my mother's funeral. Remember those two guys fighting?"

"Yes, of course."

"Well, I've only just discovered the reason for their argument. They were her lovers."

"You must have suspected that."

"Her lovers at the same time, Antoine."

"What?"

"She split her time between the two of them totally equally.

They only worked it out that day, at the cemetery. Hence their anger."

"Are you sure?"

"When we refurbished the agency offices, I came across my mother's journal. At first I wanted to destroy it, but then I read it. She explained everything in it. Her wish was to never depend on a man, but she also needed to have an affair, you remember what she was like. So she found a solution. This way, she was the one in control, and it lasted until her death. You know her own mother had been abandoned by her husband, and their first few years in Paris had been very difficult . . ."

"Why are you telling me this now?"

"When I found out, I didn't have time to tell you about it. Then this morning I remembered the funeral. Wasn't it funny?"

"The funeral?"

"Yes. The coffin stuck at an angle in the hole, those two guys at each other's throats . . ."

"The same thing happened to you, Paul."

"What do you mean?"

"Your mother was afraid you'd take up too much space in her life. So she kept you at a distance."

"You think so?"

"Of course."

There was a moment of silence. I knew he was there, and he also knew I was on the other end of the line. The highway was running past my window. I pictured him sitting in his office, alone, in the room he'd so much wanted to move into in order to be with his mother, except that she wasn't there anymore.

He wanted to tell me about that moment at the café, where we had become friends, but he was Paul, so it had to be in a roundabout way.

"I love you, Paul," I said.

"Me too, Antoine."

"Speak soon."

"Yes."

I saw Saint-Jean-Pied-de-Port appear at the bottom of a valley. There were pennants everywhere, they must have been getting ready for a local celebration. The road ran around the old town, and I had no trouble finding the sign for Esterençuby, nine kilometers away. My heart started beating faster. I was such a paradox. Even though I was fighting against anything romantic between Emma and me, I was feeling as excited as a kid at the thought of seeing her again.

The secondary road had started winding, hugging the ampleness of the landscape. The village appeared at a bend in the road. It was more a cluster of houses connected by invisible paths. It must have been nice to live here.

A bird of prey on a fence flew away as I drove by. In three flaps of its wings, it was above the church, then it flew toward the hill. The wilderness spread all around, ready to bite into the road. At night, its scouts must come down to drink from the fountains and devour the insects in the barns.

I asked for directions at the tobacconist's, which also sold newspapers and potatoes. The owner was in the process of attaching a line to a fishing rod. His face was chiseled like a rock polished by the sun and the rain. He said in a sonorous voice that the "artists" were setting up, and if I followed this road I couldn't miss them.

I let the station wagon roll at its own pace and crossed what must have been the heart of the village, a handful of houses close together, gathered around the town hall. As I drove past it, I saw a handwritten poster on the door, mentioning theater.

I thought I'd gone too far. The sign bearing the name of the place was stuck into the embankment. But then a spot of bright color attracted my attention. The red and yellow minibus was parked three bends further up; it looked like a circus van. There was just a narrow path to get to the barn, and I had all the time I needed to review what I was going to tell Emma. One, I was keeping the kiss as a gift. Two, I had thought about it at length, and I was offering her my friendship. Three, something had happened at the airport which might interest her. Four, I was proposing a pact: I would help with the tour in exchange for a few nights investigating my past.

Raphaël was the first person to see me. He was sitting outside on a table, his legs dangling, fiddling with the spotlight he had dropped in Toulouse. As soon as he saw me he straightened up, and I gathered by his attitude that he was reciting a piece inspired by my return. As I parked next to the minibus, I heard the ending. "Oh, anxious traveler, wait for the day's end to put your heart at ease . . ."

Émilie threw herself at me, and I almost fell over backwards, then Boris arrived. His ankle was bandaged, and he was leaning on a walking stick.

"I put my leg through the boards," Boris said.

"This set is a disaster," Raphaël confirmed.

They didn't look surprised to see me, as though it had been agreed from the start that I would join them after my errand at the airport.

Raphaël resumed his repair job, and Émilie and Boris went to the stage after telling me that the others were at the back. I couldn't help being nervous. I knew how Emma could lower my defenses. Going into the barn, I noticed that there were actually two buildings. The largest had the set and the auditorium, the second—which you accessed through a side door— was a large kitchen that acted as a green room for the actors. No Emma, but Victor was sitting there, at the end of the table, opposite Béatrice. She was neglecting her knitting in order to sew a large curtain that Creon was handing her in sections. They showed no surprise either, but Victor seemed gloomier than usual.

"Oh, good! Reinforcements. How about him for the guard?" he asked Béatrice.

This is how you get enlisted in the army of Thebes without anyone consulting you.

"The costume will hang loose on him."

"Not at all," Victor protested. "It'll be fine. Let's try it right away."

I followed him into the other building, keeping an eye out for Emma, beginning to find her absence strange. I was going to ask Victor where she was, but as soon as we were away from the others he beat me to it.

"Emma's in Saint-Jean," he said in confidence. "At the gendarmerie."

"What do you mean?"

He looked around to make sure nobody was listening.

"The Pessac police station called about her brother as soon as we arrived here. They found a dead body with his documents in its pockets."

"He was in a clinic . . ."

"He left early this morning, climbing over the wall. The police called their mother so she could identify the body, but she couldn't be reached. So they contacted Emma."

"Why the gendarmerie in Saint-Jean?"

"They have a scanner. The Pessac police station sent them photos so that Emma could identify her brother."

"And you let her go there alone?"

"I didn't have a choice. She made me swear not to say anything to anyone. The town hall secretary took her there."

I thought of her brother, singing in the car. His appetite at the restaurant.

"Doesn't she want to go back to Bordeaux?"

"She said it wouldn't change anything, that her brother always managed to sabotage her work. She loved him, you know."

He took my arm.

"Come and try on the costume. It's the best thing to do."

It was the complete attire of a Theban royal guard, cut to fit Boris, who must have been a good ten centimeters taller than me, but this was no time to make a fuss. I put on the tunic, then the skirt, and Victor handed me the breastplate. It was made of very thick leather, heavy to wear. It left the arms free, and the two parts closed over the chest with laces you had to tie as tightly as possible. The attire was completed with a pair of sandals, and there was also a helmet. I must admit it was very impressive, with a crest on top and ending in front with a kind of cross to protect the nose and jaw.

"You look splendid," Victor declared.

Kings are skilled at talking to the people, nothing's changed there. He rummaged in his tunic, took out his cell phone, and quickly checked the screen.

"It's her."

He picked up.

"Hi, Emma."

He listened very carefully and looked at me with eyes full of surprise, as though to make me party to astounding news.

"That's wonderful," he said to Emma. "I mean, no, it's awful for the other young man. Do they know why he had Sylvain's documents on him?"

Emma's brother must have gotten his documents stolen, or else left them as security with a dealer for whom things subsequently went wrong. I wondered where the fugitive was hiding.

"He did that?"

Emma must have been telling him where her brother was, and, judging from Victor's face, the danger seemed to recede a little more. He placed his hand on the phone and summarized the situation.

"Her brother climbed over the wall to give his mother some roses. She's taking him back to the clinic as we speak. She couldn't be reached because she inadvertently threw her cell phone into the garbage . . ." He returned to Emma, "Antoine is here. I was just talking to him . . ."

Emma interrupted him.

"I don't know," Victor replied. "He just got here. We've roped him in to play the guard to replace Boris. Alright, I'll put him on . . ."

Victor handed me his cell phone, and I got the feeling he was warning me, but of what? It was the first time I'd heard Emma's voice over the phone. Stupid, I know, but I was moved.

"Antoine?"

"Yes."

On my way to the village, I'd prepared myself for all sorts of situations. After all, I'd gotten to know her a little. I knew very well that it was possible things would not turn out exactly as I expected, but finding myself in a barn, dressed as a Theban soldier, having a conversation on which my future depended—that I had not considered.

"You must be relieved," I said, to stall for time.

"Oh, you know, he dies on a regular basis. But what are you doing there, Antoine? Weren't you supposed to catch a plane?"

Her tone was quite distant. I swallowed and climbed onto the stage to walk away from Victor.

"That's right, but something happened at the airport."

"Did you miss your flight?"

"No, I mean yes . . ."

"You sound upset."

"Emma, I have to tell you before anything else that you're very important to me."

"Is that why you decided to leave?"

"True . . . But something happened which means that I need you more than ever."

"Me?"

"Yes. Your friendship."

There was a pause.

"Are you still there?" I asked.

"And do you think I need you, Antoine?"

"In a way, yes, I suppose you do."

"In a way . . ."

"Emma, I'm going to explain everything to you—"

"Oh, no, you're not!"

"What do you mean, no?"

"Anything you like, but no explanations."

"Please, Emma . . ."

"I'm telling you no, don't insist."

There was another silence.

"I've listened to you quite a lot until now," she said, "wouldn't you agree?"

"Yes, that's true."

"Well, now it's my turn to talk. The question, Antoine, is what do you have to offer me?"

"Excuse me?"

"You heard me perfectly well."

"I told you, Emma, my friendship."

I could feel myself sweating under my helmet. I waited for a reaction from her, but it didn't come.

"Emma, are you there? I don't—"

"Didn't you like the kiss?"

"Absolutely. It was too good."

"How can a kiss be too good? Explain this to me."

I tried to free my neck from the breastplate. It was cutting into my throat.

"Because it causes a misunderstanding."

"Is what we've been through a misunderstanding?"

"Yes."

"These four days and these four nights?"

"Yes."

There was another silence, truly terrible this time, then she hung up. I froze with the phone to my ear as though I'd been turned to stone, even though this was Thebes and not Pompei. And just then, a sinister creaking sound rose from the depths of the set, you know, the kind of noise you hear in pirate movies when the bow of one of the ships guts the other.

Within a second, I saw myself sinking into this ridiculous abyss. The floorboards gave, the timber tore, and then the catastrophic movement suddenly stopped. It was obviously a momentary reprieve, so I grabbed the chance, placed my foot where the floor seemed more reliable, and, step by step, holding my breath, walked away from danger.

An emergency meeting chaired by Creon was held on the haystacks, and we decided unanimously that nobody would go back up on that stage until Raphaël had reinforced it properly. He got down to work immediately, with Émilie's help. After finding a few providential tools under a work bench, they went in search of timber in the shed.

"As for you, get to work," Victor said, brandishing the script.

He pushed his cloak back over his shoulder in order to walk more easily and made a sign for me to follow him. By the time I reacted, he was already in the middle of the field.

I hadn't noticed when I arrived, but a stream sectioned off the land below. We sat by the water. The bank was covered in rocks and shielded from the sun by chestnut trees.

"Can you help me remove this breastplate?" I said.

"Of course. You look a bit nervous."

"I'm happy to cover for Boris; but I don't know anything about theater."

"Don't you worry! It's just a game, and you only have a few lines."

Perhaps so, but he wasn't the one dressed as a soldier, about to go onstage opposite Emma.

"Let me describe the situation," he began. "The soldier you're playing has the task of watching Antigone while she's waiting to be executed. The crux of the scene is the total contrast of his state of mind with that of the heroine. Antigone is getting ready for death and is asking herself some essential questions. The guard is only concerned with his promotion and the constraints of the job. Here, take the text. I'll be Antigone."

"Can I read through my part once?"

"Of course."

I took the script from his hands, read it quickly, and we began.

"'Listen, I'm going to die soon . . . '" Victor recited.

"Do I answer?"

"Yes."

"'On the other hand,'" I read, "'people have more respect for guards than for soldiers on active service. The guard is a soldier but almost a public official.'"

"'Do you think it hurts to die?'" Victor continued.

"'I couldn't say. In the war, the soldiers who got hit in the stomach were in pain. I've never been wounded. In a way, that kept me from getting promoted.' What a bastard."

"That's not in the text, Antoine."

"Yes, but look, she's telling him—"

"Let's finish this, then we can talk about it, alright?"

"Sorry."

"I'll start again," Victor said. "'How are they going to put me to death?'"

"'I don't know. I think I heard that in order to avoid soiling the city with your blood, they're going to wall you up in a hole.'"

"'Alive?'"

"'Yes, at first.' That's awful!"

"It's the role, Antoine."

"He's just not real!"

"Oh, really? Well, I see this all the time. Indifference, self-ishness—"

"Is that how you see me, too? You think I'm a bastard?"

"What exactly are you talking about?—"

"You know perfectly well! I offered her my friendship. She hung up on me."

"You're talking about Emma."

"Of course!"

Victor sighed. "She's all or nothing."

"You could put it that way."

"Don't you want to stop fighting against yourself?"

"That's not what I'm doing!"

"You most definitely are. You're angry. And that makes you blind."

"Not at all. She's the one who's blind. She's beautiful, intelligent, young, she could have any handsome young man in the world, so what would she do with a guy like me? Tell me."

"The handsome young men, as you say, bolt the moment they see her, haven't you got that?"

"Why doesn't that surprise me?"

"She asks awkward questions. She's too demanding . . ."

"Are you talking about Antigone or Emma?"

"Same thing. Haven't you seen what goes on in the play? They all protest, cut their own throats, moan, but nobody really stands up to Creon in the end, except Antigone . . ."

"So?"

"So she sensed you were different."

"Antigone?"

"Emma."

"Oh, right. And how am I different?"

"You're not afraid."

"You must be joking. You don't know me. I'm the most frightened man in the world. I'm always running away."

"Yes, but that didn't stop you from killing him."

"Who?"

"Creon."

I understood that he was referring to her father.

"Actually, he did that on his own."

"It takes killing him to be able to say that, and I don't mean you murdered him."

He was looking at me with the expression of a king who'd seen other clumsy guards, foot soldiers of denial who were forever evading the issue.

I lowered my head.

"You're right," I conceded.

"Well . . ."

I picked up a pebble and threw it in the stream.

"I'm angry because I can't give her what she wants."

"You can't, or you won't?"

"I can't."

"Why not?"

"She scares me."

"And yet you're still here."

"That's for a different reason. A personal problem I need to sort out."

He listened carefully. He waited. I made a gesture to avoid the question.

"It's too complicated."

"It's yourself you're scared of," Victor said. "That's the only issue."

I looked, beyond the trees, at the light advancing on the field in step with the clouds. The landscape was constantly changing.

We sat in silence for a moment. The stream continued its course, the wind stirred the branches. I tried to remember the way Herbie Hancock hit the keys and wondered where the sparkles in the water came from, back on the pontoon in Cap-Martin. Would my life ever stop escaping me? There were so many things crowding my brain.

"It's true," I admitted. "I'm the one who's scared. She's done nothing but reach out to me from the start."

"Scared of what, Antoine?"

I sighed.

"If only I knew."

We went back to the barn. Raphaël and Émilie had almost finished repairing the stage. They'd used all the wood supply and reinforced the floor in as many places as possible. As for Boris, he'd taken it upon himself to make the kitchen usable. It wasn't that he lacked utensils or the necessities for setting a table, but everything was covered in dust. I offered my help as dish washer while he dried up. We were a good team.

The sound of an engine grew closer, something ancient, like a 2CV. There still are some in the countryside, and they're still very good.

"It's Emma coming back from Saint-Jean," Boris said.

I heard her talking to Victor outside, then she came into the kitchen. She'd taken advantage of her trip into town to buy wine, coffee, and chocolate.

"Did you find what you were looking for?" Boris asked.

"No, but no big deal."

She'd had to give an excuse to conceal her visit to the gendarmerie, the need just to buy something or other. She finished putting down her shopping as though I weren't there, and went back out.

"Lovers' tiff?" Boris asked.

I would have happily strangled him, and picked up the pace to prevent him from making other comments.

Béatrice joined us shortly afterwards. She looked at us, washing up like crazy, the limping giant and the Theban soldier.

"You're both so cute."

"Aren't we just?" Boris said.

"I'm afraid I'm going to take your partner in crime away. We're setting up, now that the stage has been reinforced."

Béatrice gave me half an hour to learn my lines, and once I knew them by heart, I went into the other building. Emma was already in position. She was repeating her part softly, dressed in that ocher dress I'd seen her rehearse in back in Toulouse, and I got the same shock.

I put on my helmet and went up onto the stage. In some ways, I was glad I was wearing this warrior's disguise under which I could hide a little.

Béatrice gave us our marks and showed us the moves to reach them, which were minimal, and we began. Emma looked at me harshly, it was the first thing I noticed, and her voice was cold. When it was my turn to respond to her, I heard myself speak, but it was mechanical, my mind was elsewhere. I was looking at her, shut up in my armor, and it was all I could do. Behind every word of hers, her slightest gesture, I felt she was angry with me.

Béatrice let us get to the end of the text. There. It was over already.

"Well done for learning your lines so quickly, Antoine," she started by saying.

I couldn't take any credit. Working on screenplays constantly forced me to juggle with words and sentences. You always had some in your mind, and I was good at it, storing up, reproducing.

"However, neither of you are taking this in the right direction," she continued. "Emma, you look like you're judging him when he's just a guard. What you're going through is a little over his head. He protects himself by talking about his promotion. He's clinging to tangible realities. Your expression is too harsh. One should feel that, on some level, you understand him. He's just a man. You, you want to defy the gods. That's your business. As a matter of fact, it's what the character says—"

"'You'll find your peace of mind again,'" Emma said from memory. "'It's okay.'"

"That's right," Béatrice confirmed. "Deep inside her, Antigone knows that her demands are out of the ordinary . . ."

Emma listened, arms crossed. Gradually, her face lost some of its harshness. She was agreeing. Béatrice turned to me.

"Antoine, same thing but in reverse. You can't say these lines and keep this respectful, even worshipful attitude, toward her. It's impossible. The last thing the guard wants is to worship her, it would be going too far. He prefers to keep his feet firmly on the ground. He's the perfect illustration of the way we protect ourselves when we're overwhelmed by an event . . ."

It was cruelly true. This play had been written specially for me.

"Hey, guys, can you give us a hand?"

Boris suddenly appeared from the barn. A truck had come to deliver what the village was giving us as a thank you for our visit, but it had stayed down there on the road, because the path was too narrow. We all went down to meet it. It was bringing enough food for an army on the field. And that wasn't all. The mayor, who was driving the truck, announced that a farm uphill was giving us half a pig. We just had to go get it.

"I'll go," I spontaneously offered.

I needed to go for a drive. The mayor drew me a rough map on a sheet of paper torn out of an exercise book. The farm was less than five kilometers away, once you were past the hill, but I wished it were on the other side of the planet.

I got into the Passat and was ready to start it up when Emma approached.

"Béatrice is right, you know," she said simply.

She was talking about the acting, about Antigone and the guard, but it was all mixed together.

"Antigone is so . . . so absolute," she added. "And he's just a man."

All the severity she'd had since her return from Saint-Jean was gone.

6

I left the last houses behind me and drove much faster than appropriate on these mountain roads. Life was mocking me. I'd spent all these years building a world adapted to what life could offer when you were wise enough to turn away from what it denied you. Simple pleasures made me happy and too bad if people thought I wasn't driven enough, I did not harbor resentment, let alone envy. I kept away from everything excessive, violent, complex, and had my share of everything, bad things included. I couldn't say that nothing serious would ever happen to me, but I think I was able to picture even a disaster as a mere fact, accept it, and overcome it. Everything had gone well for me until now. But fate, that trickster, had prepared something special for my kind of self-sufficiency. There were small roles in a movie, easy to delete, and it so happened that the producer was trying to cut certain costs to make up for his rounds in a helicopter and maritime parties. So he asked me to make the necessary alterations, I was the right person for this kind of mission, a real gun for hire, except that this time I'd shot myself in the foot.

The road was cut into the side of the mountain, and I could see the sequence of bends as far as the pass. The poor Passat was twisting, moaning, giving its engine's all.

I saw myself back in my hotel room in Cap Martin, making my cuts with that detachment I was so proud of and the speed that ensured I could have a nice time. I even remember the content of that modest scene in which Emma was going to play the waitress and highlight the cruelty of a Mafioso. And I could almost hear my fingers tapping on the computer keyboard, pressing SELECT then DELETE. When was that again? How many years ago?

At the top of the pass, the road forked, as indicated on the mayor's map. In order to reach the Buru farm, I had to turn right and drive onto the plateau.

I'd erased one page, two perhaps, in a screenplay that would in no way alter movie history, but what an upheaval it had triggered in my own life. That there should be Emma Cassentis in this world, that you could feel quite comfortable with another person, actually somewhat like with yourself, that it should be possible to share the most intimate, truest part of yourself, and, above all, a part you didn't know existed, that was something I'd never foreseen, me the great shorts-wearing strategist. 6-0, 6-0, 6-0, that's what life had shoved at me, just to put me back in my place, that of a small-time player. But wasn't it typical of the human condition to get a thrashing on the court before having your name engraved in marble above the bar at a provincial club? "Here, Antoine Maupas was thwarted; he attempted nothing, so lost everything."

I knew other smart asses like me. That was it, after all. Rick Blaines so concerned with keeping their white jackets pristine that they preferred to let an Ingrid Bergman leave with a guy she didn't love anymore, just to be "classy." There were even those who managed to be heroic without saving anyone, those were the best, sons of Creon who'd plunge a dagger into their stomachs before their poor father's very eyes just to have the final say, instead of digging a secret exit in their Antigone's cave and taking her far away from Thebes, to a world where you're allowed to say no. What a merry band of losers we were—not that there was anything to be proud of. After that, how could we be surprised that Rahan should have such a high rating? And Batman and the whole gang of superheroes? That our kids should buy knives to be less afraid of the dark?

The Buru farm. It was there, on the left. A sign indicated the road that led to it, well . . . when I say road . . . it was rather a country lane that soon turned into a simple dirt path with deep ruts. I drove into a forest of fir trees all close together and suddenly felt as though I was entering another world. The sky was so dark that it was as though night had fallen prematurely, and the landscape looked seeped in mystery. The suspension was hitting the ground so much that I was forced to drive in second gear. I forded a stream and, on the other side, saw the farm, it had to be it, there was no other house for kilometers. There was a contained power emanating from it, though I couldn't put my finger on it. Perhaps it was the granite wall rising behind it, as though the human world stopped there.

A silhouette appeared on the path, by the large gates. It was a child of ten or so. He must have seen me from a distance and made a sign for me to drive straight into the farmyard, which was very large. Apparently, here you could take up as much space as you needed.

I parked outside the house, which had narrow windows and thick walls, and a huge black dog put its paws on the car door.

"Igurb!" the boy cried. "Come here!"

The dog let me get out of the car then started running toward its master. Standing on its hind legs, it was as tall as him.

"He's good," the boy added, meaning that the dog; was friendly for a seventy-kilogram beast. He proffered his hand. He was as beautiful as the nature around him. Hairy, luminous, also exuding the mystery that was probably inherited if you were born on this plateau.

"My name is Uztai. And I know who you are. We have to go get it."

"What?"

"The pig."

"Oh."

"Animals feel it when they're going to be killed. But it's not far. We'll catch it with Imanol. It'll be easy with three of us."

So we were about to kill the pig—this Imanol I'd not yet seen, the kid, and I. The day had been trying enough already, and I can't say I was enthused by the prospect of a rodeo at high altitude, but I didn't let on.

A volley of words suddenly hit us. An old woman was coming toward us. She was very short, as though flattened by a giant's fist, and her front teeth were missing. She spoke a thick Basque. Words poured out of her mouth like a stream hurtling between stones.

"This is my grandmother Zaraitzu," the child said, pointing at her.

Zaraitzu gave orders, and the child translated. It was the way they operated. This woman looked like an apron-clad general defending his lands.

"We'll give you boots," Uztai translated. "She's asking where you come from, she means the country, because of what you're wearing."

"Oh, this—it's for a play."

The grandmother spat on the ground and asked another question.

"She's asking the title."

"Of the play? *Antigone*."

"She's an expert, you know."

A tall beanpole came out of the shed where the farming equipment was stored. Imanol, I supposed. He must have been at least two meters tall, taking the record away from Boris. He undulated rather than walked, like the stem of a plant pinched

208 · ALAIN GILLOT

between your fingers, and had huge, leaf-like hands. The grandmother called him abruptly, and he wiped his forehead as he answered her. He looked a little put out.

"Imanol says the pig is at the barrier," Uztai translated again.

We went into the house, which smelled of wood and ashes—they must have lit the fire even in the summer—and while I was trying on the rubber boots spiders had turned into their nest, the grandmother pointed at a picture above the fireplace, and the kid rushed to take it down.

"It's Saint Bernarde!" he exclaimed, shoving the photo under my nose. "She saved my grandmother's mother."

I knew that face. There was another, tiny photo, also under glass and placed at the very bottom of the frame. It was so damaged that you had to come up very close to see it clearly. It was the same woman, on stage, dressed as the Lady of the Camelias.

"It's Sarah Bernhardt," I said, feeling as smug as though I'd just won a gameshow on TV.

The grandmother shook her head, and the stream resumed its speed, flooding the entire room with words. Then she suddenly stopped so that Uztai could translate.

"This woman," Uztai proudly explained, "saw my grandmother's mother at the Bordeaux hospital. She had no money, and no surgeon wanted to operate on her, and this woman took care of everything and saved her. My grandmother has a book about her. She'll show it to you."

I now understood better what connected them to actors. But what was Imanol doing? I heard a rustling sound from the small room behind the kitchen. Imanol emerged, all smiles, with a set of knives of different sizes that he'd just sharpened. The bell had tolled for the pig.

The three of us cut quite a figure—the child carrying a rope with a ready-made slipknot, for catching the animal, I imagined;

Imanol with his club over his shoulder, I figured in guise of local anesthetic; and me, the Theban soldier, makeshift killer at best. We hadn't even reached the far end of the farmyard when large drops began to fall on us, and the weather heralded a thunderstorm.

The barrier Imanol had referred to closed off the family property on the mountainside. In order to reach it, you had to walk three hundred meters across a field that must have served as pasture for the sheep.

We approached the pig, which was showing us its rump and seemed to be ignoring us, but of course that wasn't true, and when we were less than thirty meters away, it began to move, scampering along at first, then, when we spread out around it, running a little faster. Although I was no pig-hunting expert, I got the feeling that this representative of the porcine species was far from having lost the match. It had space before it, could alter its speed depending on ours, and had the weather on its side. The heavier it rained, the more advantage hooves had over boots. It was going to take us hours. That's when it turned around, against all expectations, and tried to take us from the rear and outflank us on the wing by using the gap between the barrier and us.

Why was it taking this risk? Was it bravado? Did it think it could leave the farm on this side? Go figure.

It was now rushing at me, and I realized I had no choice but to tackle it. I tried to remember my amateur-rugby reflexes, looked for my support, bent my knees, spread my arms in full, but it was going too fast, was too strong, and literally catapulted me backwards so I ended up on my front. I was a mediocre pig hunter, I had to admit. I tried to get up but slid back into the mud. I wanted to apologize to my partners for failing in my role, but, at the same time, I saw the demise of the powerful animal take place before my astonished eyes.

The pig had humiliated me, of course, but in our rough collision, it had also lost its balance and fallen on its side a little farther away. In other circumstances, it might have gotten back up with a push of the loins, but the slippery ground that had first given it an advantage now spelled its ruin. It was desperately trying to get back up, its legs whipping the air, in vain, and Uztai had all the time he needed to capture it as Imanol slowly raised his club and brought it down between the animal's eyes.

It was over. Without even a start. And while the kid was retrieving his rope, the giant put his hand on the animal's forehead, as though to apologize.

"Well played!" Uztai shouted, turning toward me.

He wanted to be kind, but he wasn't taken in, of that I was sure, and I planned to tell him so as soon as I managed to get back up on my feet. I put my weight on one leg, and when I pushed on it in order to straighten up, an excruciating pain shot through my back, and I collapsed. What was happening to me? I was literally nailed to the ground. I'd never been in so much pain in my life, and I was sure that if I moved again, even just wriggled my toe, I would feel the same awful pain, and that was something I didn't want to experience for all the world.

Imanol approached, then his brother. They looked at me. I opened my mouth, but no sound came out.

"Imanol," Uztai finally said, "go fetch the cart. I'll stay here with him."

The human mind is a funny thing. At that moment, while crucified in the mud as though cut in half, my chief concern was my outfit. How could I possibly have kept my skirt and breastplate to go and pick up this pig on the mountain? I'd have to go back in time to understand.

It had all happened so fast. I'd seen this mountain mission as a way of escaping from rehearsing with Emma and had darted into the station wagon to flee her gaze because I thought my confusion was so obvious.

It's always our emotions that push us to accomplish irrational acts, I guess the way it happens during a hold-up, or when you serve the ball in tennis, or when you strangely start reorganizing your closets, in Bordeaux, after your child goes missing.

Imanol came back with the cart, and it took them a good fifteen minutes to heave me onto it using some sort of stretcher. Then they put the pig next to me much less carefully. Our strange crew started making its way back to the farm, and I looked at the companion of my misfortune lying next to me. There was no mark on its forehead; it just looked asleep, and its long ginger eyelashes made it look sweet.

The grandmother was standing outside the house. When she saw us coming, she opened the door wide so that the stretcher could fit through. Her grandsons put me on the table while waiting to make me a bed, but I asked them not to move me. I had some experience of lumbago and knew that, in these circumstances, the best thing to do was lie on a hard, flat surface.

Imanol disappeared with his large knife, and I assumed he'd gone to deal with the pig while Uztai and his grandmother started a conversation, in Basque, of course, until the kid nodded and suddenly left the house.

They'd decided something, but what? I tried to organize my thoughts. There must be a physiotherapist in Saint-Jean, who could at least give me some relief before I went back to the barn. I thought the best thing would be to call an ambulance and was waiting for Uztai to come back so that I could tell him, but when he reappeared he didn't even give me a chance to speak.

"Agustin will be here soon. The dog's gone to fetch him."

My initial reaction was to sit up and reply, but the pain nailed me to the table. That was exactly what I had to avoid doing.

Giving in to impulse. I had to stay calm and not say or do anything without having thought it through carefully first, to push away stress and think positively. Things were bound to work out.

"Who's Agustin?" I asked.

"A wizard," Uztai replied.

7

Uztai was sitting cross-legged on the large table and was holding the photo album open before me. He was concentrating very hard since he had to turn the pages and at the same time translate Zaraitzu's commentary, which led me through her family's past.

Her mother, Lezana, had been hospitalized in Bordeaux because of a brain tumor. We must realize that back in 1920 this was a frightening operation, and not just for the patient. Many surgeons shied away from performing surgery on this risky area, fearing that failure would damage their reputation. Now, it so happened that the great Sarah Bernhardt was in that same hospital at the time to have a gangrenous leg amputated. It was in those dramatic circumstances that she befriended Lezana. She then asked her own surgeon to perform the operation, for which she paid herself and which turned out to be successful. Ever since, the home of the Etchegaray family had been open to entertainers and, even now, whenever a theater company passed through the region, a pig would be sacrificed to it.

Imanol came back from the barn. His forearms were covered in blood, and he threw into the sink all sorts of cutting utensils that evoked a rather different kind of operation than the one he'd just performed.

Agustin Mendiburu would be here soon, and I could clearly see in the faces of my hosts that they didn't doubt for a second that he would manage to put me right again. For my part, I was more pragmatic. My knowledge of native populations all over the world led me to accept their "wizard's" intervention without batting an eyelid, even though I harbored no illusions about his gifts. But his failure had to be blatantly obvious before they would agree to call an ambulance.

The dog entered the room first, with Agustin in his wake, and I think that in other circumstances I would have burst out laughing. While we were waiting for this man who seemed to impress them so much, I'd formed a certain idea of this mountain practitioner, whom they also called the "Borodze Mage." I'd imagined a striking man with coal-black eyes and calloused hands, churning out spells rather than words, something like a hermit. However, in no way did Agustin fit this description. The best way I could portray him is as an American tourist coming off a cruise, and when he came close to me, I thought he was going to sell me a group ticket for a week in the Caribbean.

"What's your name, my boy?" he asked.

"Antoine."

He sounded like Joe Pesci in *Goodfellas*—I mean that's the kind of trust he inspired—and was wearing a Hawaiian shirt decorated with coconut trees on small sandy islands surrounded by a blue ocean, but that wasn't all. His hair was dyed a kind of blonde that edged on ginger in places, and on his hairy wrist, he wore a watch as huge as it was ridiculous.

"You'll need to take your clothes off and turn over," he said. "I know you think you can't do it, but it won't be a problem, you'll see."

My approach to native populations had its limits, I realized at that moment. Accepting their beliefs was all very good, but this operetta wizard could actually cripple me. How could this family, who seemed steeped in common sense, trust a man in a Hawaiian shirt?

"Let me know when you're ready."

"To sit up?"

"Yes."

"I can't."

"Yes, you can. Just ask your body to do it, and I'll help you."

My inner voice was screaming at me not to obey, but I didn't listen to it. This much power he did have. And, strangely enough, I sat up, I'd almost say effortlessly.

"There we go," he simply remarked.

How had he managed this magic trick? If he wasn't a doctor, then he was at least a little bit of a sorcerer.

"Now we're going to take this breastplate off, if you don't mind."

He made a sign to Uztai to come and help him free me from the costume.

"Now let me know when you're ready to turn over."

This time I was going to observe carefully, as there had to be a rational explanation.

"I'm ready."

But once again it happened so quickly that I learned nothing new. At most, he had accompanied my movement. It was a little unsettling, though.

Then he started to talk with the farm residents, and from that moment on, it was impossible to doubt his Basque origins, given the speed and power of his delivery, and, in a single motion, the three Etchegarays left the house, accompanied by the dog.

It was just the two of us now, and the moment of truth was approaching. I felt sweat running down my forehead. I was wrong to worry. All I was risking was lifelong paralysis.

I heard water pouring into the sink. Agustin must have been washing his hands. Then he approached me and put the tips of his fingers on the top of my spine. I closed my eyes. Here we go.

"Tell me if it hurts, alright?"

"Alright."

He began his tactile exploration. The pressure of his fingers was steady and in no way painful. He would pause, then resume his movement, and he reached the tip of my sacrum in the same way, without my feeling any discomfort. After which, he walked away and emitted a kind of stifled growl, which I took to mean he was puzzled. This was perhaps my last chance to regain my advantage, and I leaped into the breach.

"You know," I said in a voice full of humility, "I didn't want to disturb you. They're the ones who decided to call you. I wanted to call an ambulance."

I waited for his answer, but it didn't come. It was as though he hadn't heard me. There was the sound of a pan, of dishes. Was he concocting a mixture now? Was I now going to meet the wizard? No. Nothing of the sort. I realized from the smell that he was making coffee, and, shortly afterwards, he came to sit a little distance from the table, facing me, holding a cup.

"Have you had this pain before, Antoine?"

"Yes, but never this severe."

"When?"

"I play a lot of tennis and sometimes don't warm up enough. Or else I don't take tiredness into account properly. In that case, my back sometimes jams, more or less seriously."

Agustin was drinking small sips. He was watching me.

"What kind of tiredness do you mean? General tiredness or linked to a specific event?"

"I write, and that's a lot more physical than people think."

"And have you been feeling tired lately?"

"Yes, a little. I've been traveling."

"Ah . . ."

I expected him to ask more questions, but he remained silent. He finished his coffee, got up, and walked out of sight again. I then didn't hear him for a good ten minutes. I thought of the others, of the barn. They must have been worried.

Sarah Bernhardt was looking at me from the fireplace. I was

in a truly singular situation, and it couldn't go on. I had to take back the initiative. I started to put together words in my head to ask Agustin, as tactfully as possible, to call an ambulance, but, all of a sudden, although I thought he was on the other side of the room, he took hold of my left foot and pressed the arch, at a very specific spot. It was as though he was ramming an iron rod into my foot and it was slowly going up my leg. That's the best way I can describe what I felt at that moment. Unimaginable pain. My entire body became the center of this pain, which radiated out, took over every centimeter of my flesh, laid siege to my brain, and I thought I would lose my mind.

That's when the memory appeared. So clearly that it almost wasn't a memory but a situation I was living through in the present.

I was in my parents' house, aged five. Normally, I should have been at school, but I'd woken up feeling ill, and my mother had asked my grandmother to look after me while she was at work. At one stage, I'd escaped her watch and ventured out of my room in pajamas, barefoot, finally reaching the door of the garage, my favorite place. I'd go there whenever I could, get into the car, and sit behind the wheel. I couldn't see anything, but I could smell the scent of car journeys, and I liked that. The door was ajar, which surprised me, because our father would always tell us off if he found a door hadn't been shut. I wanted to get into the car, like the other times, but as I pushed down on the handle, I heard a noise that alarmed me coming from the other side of the car. I let go of the handle and walked around the hood. My father was there, with a woman who wasn't my mother, lifting her in small jolts, as she stood flat against the wall. It all looked rather odd, and I felt a little uneasy. What I found most surprising was that my father's pants were down and I could see his underpants around his calves. Silly, I know, but I'd never seen my father

218 · ALAIN GILLOT

in underpants, he was very modest, and I felt embarrassed. I made for the garage exit as softly as I could. I was nearly there when I stepped on something, a nail, a screw, I don't know, but the pain was so sharp that I had to make an unimaginable effort not to cry out, and I ran and hid in the bathroom, where I stayed shut away, shaking from top to toe, until I managed to control myself.

I screamed with all my strength. In the present. I think the farm walls must have shaken because of this cry that had been deep inside me all these years, and that's when they all came back in, Uztai, his grandmother, Imanol, and the dog. They helped Agustin hold me down while I struggled, wept, and uttered incomprehensible words, and, gradually, exhausted myself, stopped moving altogether, my mouth open and my eyes wild. Then they let go of me and left the room again, except for Agustin, and we remained there in a charged silence.

"Perhaps you could try to walk?" he finally said.

"What?"

"I said you could try to walk."

Nothing could surprise me at this stage, and, as a matter of fact, when I put my feet on the floor, I had no trouble standing or taking a few steps. The pain had disappeared. I walked to the end of the room, then returned to Agustin. He seemed lost in his own thoughts, as though what had just happened was perfectly ordinary.

"What did you do?" I asked.

He had his back to me. He was washing his hands carefully, then he dried them.

"I don't know if you'll believe me, but I had nothing to do with it."

"What do you mean?"

"You did everything yourself."

8

gustin was slipping his wrist back into the watch that was so vulgar it had given me the impression—along with other details—that I was dealing with a barker, or worse, a dangerous crook. I was still standing opposite him, trying to understand.

"Seriously, though . . ." I said.

"Seriously," Agustin said, "I didn't do anything because there's nothing wrong with you."

"I don't understand . . . You saw the state I was in when you arrived."

He sighed. He must have been through this many times and didn't care for explanations. Still, he made an effort.

"That pain was connected to a trauma. On a conscious level, you'd forgotten it, but it was still there, and your unconscious was expressing it through pain."

I tried to recap.

"Yes, but . . . There's still something wrong with my foot . . ."

"No."

"No?"

"You had your pain, that's all. Your foot could have been pierced through, but there's nothing left of it now. Except a memory."

"Has my pain gone forever?"

"Yes, because you've acknowledged what it was trying to tell you. So it has no more reason to exist."

"So there's nothing wrong with my back, either?"

220 - ALAIN GILLOT

"No. It was just the body compensating that caused the pain in the spine. The foot is often responsible for this kind of lumbago. Our relationship with the ground is fundamental."

I watched him as we spoke. We were on this farm. In the middle of the mountains. I was to remember forever that a man with that kind of shirt, who dyed his hair like that, could actually be extremely competent. Even if I couldn't understand his method, let alone his conclusions. I felt the need to cling to something rational.

"How much do I owe you?" I heard myself say, the way you do in a specialist's office.

He smiled.

"I don't work for money, Antoine, I have too much of it already. Wherever I've been in the world, I've taken care of people who keep sending me money, they can't help themselves, and I have more than enough. They think they have to pay in order not to suffer, but that's not the case. Do you understand? We have the right to be pain-free. By the way, my watch comes from a funfair."

"Excuse me?'

"I see you've been looking at it for a while. It puzzles you, doesn't it? My nephew gave it to me. He won it at one of those stalls, you know, where you fish things out with claws. Obviously, it doesn't show the time, it's a toy, but it says my nephew to me; it's another kind of temporal reference point."

At that moment, I understood just what an idiot I'd been, and how patient he'd been with me. There I was, struggling with my fears, my prejudice, and he had been kind enough to free me from my pain.

"Do you live here?" I asked.

"A few months a year. I also have a house in Florida."

Basically, I'd been wrong about everything.

"But I prefer it here. It's quiet."

When we came out, there was a menacing thunderclap, and a large flash of lightning tore through the sky.

"Mind the bear on your way back," Agustin said. "I saw her when I was coming here. She can be unpredictable when there's a storm."

"A bear?"

"Yes. Her name's Laura. She's already knocked a truck into the ravine."

The rain grew heavier, and I had to rush. After thanking them all, I hugged them, even Imanol, even the dog, and returned to my car.

I skidded a little as I left the farm, jolted over a little bump, and heard a thump behind me. It was the pig.

I wanted just one thing, and that was to zoom through these few kilometers and be back at the barn, but I had to be reasonable. At all costs, avoid breaking the suspension or driving into a ravine. I had what it took to make a feast, I had what it took to look Emma in the eye, take her in my arms, and kiss her. I'd believed myself to be incapable of loving, but that wasn't the case, I'd been lied to, which was a very different matter.

It wasn't what I'd seen in the garage that had traumatized me, it was what had happened subsequently, that is, nothing special. Life at home had simply resumed its course. My mother had come home from work. My father, who'd meanwhile gone to his job—he was doing night shifts in the factory—only came back the next day, and we'd had a meal like any other. We didn't speak at the table, our hands had to be clean, and we couldn't get up without permission. And then, when it was bedtime, I'd heard my parents go into their bedroom and shut the door behind them. What did they talk about in that room? Did they talk about the woman in the garage? Did my mother know? The following day, my father had put on his coat, checked he had his papers and canteen pass, and I realized that the following days would all be the

222 · ALAIN GILLOT

same, that there would never be a word, a sign, that I was excluded from their lives forever and we were condemned to act out this comedy for all eternity.

The rain wasn't easing off, and the level of the stream had risen considerably. I sped into it, the water spraying on both sides of the car. Then I went through the little wood of fir trees, and, when I emerged, I felt as though I were leaving a secret realm.

It wasn't the fact that my father had had an affair with a lady that had been difficult. He might as well have blown himself up with three Senegalese infantrymen, for all I cared. Ask any child in the world, and they'll all answer the same thing. What a child wants is to see his parents happy, no matter how, to share this happiness with them, not to be left outside the door. That damned closed door outside which I'd waited all these years.

I felt the asphalt under my wheels. I'd gotten back onto the secondary road. The weather was getting worse and worse, I couldn't see a great deal, the windshield wipers couldn't cope, but that wasn't all. I was crying, for the first time in my life, and I couldn't stop.

Years' worth of tears were pouring out, years of repressed emotions, thousands of dance steps and bursts of laughter, and then all those middle-of-the-night hot chocolates I'd missed, all the hands I hadn't held, and all those meals with white tablecloths I hadn't attended, and children playing under the table, all the families I'd denied myself. Everything I'd kept inside, like a nail I'd swallowed, in order not to cry out.

I was weeping, yes, at last, and I was laughing. I was laughing because I was weeping.

9

I can't have been very far from the pass. It was night in broad daylight, but with every flash of lightning, every-thing became visible for a second, and I had to take advan-tage of it to find my bearings.

I now understood why I'd run away from kindergarten, why I couldn't stand that ordinary little drama at the airport, why in general I'd always managed to avoid the adult world. I didn't want to grow up because it was a prison, and there was bound to be a lie behind it. I didn't want to hide in a garage, I didn't want to put on every morning the coat of bitterness my father had always worn. I now understood why. I didn't want to be incapable of sharing with my family, and carry this failure with me to work, and come back in the evening and complain that the soup was cold, that my children had worn out the tips of their shoes a little too soon, or that there were too many mosques. I didn't want to grow up because that meant lying to others and, therefore, to myself.

It's not that I was judging my parents, but I didn't want to be like them. Behind this moment of pleasure, at least I hope it was, in a garage, there were so many self-denials, so much refusal to laugh, to relax, on a daily basis. Of course you had to shut the doors in that house, of course you shouldn't talk too much. Lies need internal adjustments and silence. If we had opened those doors, invited friends over, danced, sung, perhaps in a moment of drunkenness, with a look, a gesture, everything would've been discovered, who knows? It was bet-ter to be sad, it was more prudent.

I now remembered another moment that had puzzled me, when my mother had said to one of my sisters, with regard to sex, "You'll see, it's just an unpleasant moment to get through." Obviously, they'd come to an understanding in the bedroom. After all, it was their business, but then they also had the business of us, their children, to bequeath us a smile, some laissez-faire, the odd morning. It's called tenderness, I think; I've heard of it. I suddenly remembered that I'd never jumped into their bed, like all children do, I think, on a Sunday, at the risk of being told off, in search of a cuddle, a moment to look up at the ceiling, make shadows with their hands, to tell stories laying against the warmth of their mothers' bellies or their fathers' arms. That's where your infidelity lay, my dear dad. The other one, in the garage, I would have happily granted you, had I not missed you so much. And—shit, I was out of gas.

You always get caught out this way. I'd even told myself as I left Toulouse, "Fill up while you're on the highway," but I was in a rush to arrive. Then, once I was on the national road, I'd missed the gas station while overtaking a truck, and then, since I'd almost reached my destination, I'd decided to go later.

I rocked the Passat a little but could only go another hundred meters or so and parked beside the muddy slope. It was silly. The pass 'couldn't have been very much farther, and if I could have reached it, then I would have simply freewheeled down.

I got out of the car and noticed it had sunk a little. I tried pushing it but in vain. There was nothing else for me to do but walk. So be it. It was just a mishap, and it would have taken more than that to discourage me. Especially so close to my goal. Especially now that I had no more screws or nails in my foot. I could picture the actors busying themselves on the stage and in the kitchen. I wanted to see their faces when I laid the pig at their feet.

I opened the trunk and pulled the carcass toward me, but as I was about to heave it up, I thought I should first put on my costume. I now had a responsibility, however small, in this play. I had to bring back not just the pig but also the soldier. So I put on the breastplate and tied it as best I could. It wasn't going to be as comfortable but, on the other hand, it was protection against rain, and when I put the half pig over my shoulder, I felt it settle comfortably on the leather reinforcement.

A flash of lightning lit up the plateau. If I cut across the fields instead of going as far as the pass, I would already save a lot of time. I found a balance in the way I carried my load and stuck to it. On the other hand, I got rid of my sandals. They were hurting me, and I'd always preferred to walk barefoot.

I thought of the pain I'd felt in that garage. It was the fact that I'd stopped myself from crying out that had made it so strong, because once I'd examined my arch when I was shut in the bathroom, I'd seen that the wound wasn't very deep. Over the next few days, however, I'd had trouble walking, and my mother had taken me to the pharmacy, saying that my foot didn't "look nice." I'd even been entitled to an anti-tetanus jab and a nice bandage, but I'd felt no more discomfort and, on the contrary, had even been pleased to have had this little accident because my mother had been forced to take care of me. It's not that she didn't love us, but she had a lot of work and did at least three jobs at once, seamstress, market vendor, housewife, so when exactly would she have had time to put her children in her lap? But it wasn't just that, it was also that puzzling reserve of hers, that fear of showing what she felt. Now I understood better why. She must have taken on so much to look after this "decent" family until cancer took her away with her secret. During this time, her husband, on the other side of the partition wall, unable to hold her hand, was busy growing his tumor.

They'd really hurt each other, those two, and also us, their children. They should have opened the garage instead. Cars are made to be driven.

I reached the extremity of the plateau and saw the valley open up before me, with the stream twisting beneath. When I looked carefully, I could almost make out the barn, in front of the first houses. I resumed walking with tenfold energy, I almost couldn't feel my load, my back was strong and my hamstrings supple, and the storm couldn't do anything to me and was in the process of giving up, anyway.

I crossed the road and went down the slope that led straight to the stream, a smile on my lips. In the end, it was much better to come back this way rather than freewheeling it. I hadn't broken down, quite the contrary. That's when I saw her, the aforementioned Laura. I'd forgotten all about her. She was standing on her hind legs, sniffing the wind, about fifty meters away. She must have been watching me for a little while, and I comforted myself with the thought that, had she wanted to attack me, she would have done it by now.

I kept my eyes fixed on the stream and repeated the basics to myself, such as keep walking at the same pace, look ahead, and avoid any reaction that the bear could interpret as fear. Rightly or wrongly, I saw the stream as a natural ally and managed to persuade myself that if I could reach it and cross it, she would definitely not follow me.

I remembered being in a similar situation in Africa. On our way back from filming a sequence with birds in the Okavango Delta, we came across a lion. We'd lost track of time in our eagerness to bring back footage at all costs, even though our guide had advised us to return in daylight, while predators were still asleep. The lion had followed us for a while, and we had our hearts in our boots, even though we had a shotgun. When we arrived within sight of the village where we'd erected our camp, he had stopped abruptly at a line of dense scrub, and our guide told us that he always did that, even though he could have easily gotten over the obstacle. I was hoping that the stream would have the same effect on the bear.

As I was approaching the waterway, I couldn't help turning to look. Perhaps that's what prompted her. Or had she decided the moment she saw me walk onto the field? In any case, the bear began to move.

I felt a wave of heat rush over my body, and I picked up the pace.

The stream was a little wider here than outside the barn, and deeper. I went into the water, careful not to slip on the pebbles, in particular not wanting to let go of my trophy. I felt the cold water seep under my breastplate, weighing it down, but I held on and put my foot on the opposite bank.

I could now make out the barn clearly. There was smoke coming out of the chimney, Boris must have made a fire in order to have embers, in anticipation of the pig.

I resumed my walk ahead, but that's when I heard a stifled growl, a little too close for my liking. I had to accept the evidence that the animal had crossed the stream, too. What could I do? Get rid of the pig? I considered it, of course, but I couldn't accept the prospect. These moments show human nature. The castaway who keeps his watch, the survivor who goes back for his boots in a house on fire, and I thought of Emma and her ideas about pride. I'd come too long a way, too far, to abandon my catch to the playground bully. I was happy to grant her part of it, but for that I would have needed something to cut with, and I'd left my sword on the stage. You could tell how inexperienced I was. A Theban soldier, a real one, would never have parted from his weapon.

I picked up the pace considerably through the field, now just a pool of mud after all that had poured down from the sky.

The bear growled a second time, more clearly, which meant she had come closer, and what I felt rise within me was not fear, it was too late for that, but huge anger, and I suddenly turned around to face her.

I think the animal was even more surprised than I was. I could tell by the way she slowed down, then stopped to sniff the air. She must have been trying to collect information about this odd behavior on the part of a human with no weapon and in the dark. Was I going to run at her? Get out a lasso? She was undecided as to how to act, and I felt that it was now or never. I took a step forward and shouted at her with all my strength, practically bursting my lungs, and it so happened that at that very moment a flash of lightning tore through the sky like a paroxysm of fury. It was crunch time. The bear was close enough to me to have annihilated me in three strides and a blow from her paw. It was too late to make a run for it, and I had ample time to study her. She really was a splendid animal that must have weighed close to three hundred kilograms. She growled, louder than the other times, and I told myself this was the end, that Paul would never know what I'd come to this valley for, that he would always wonder what I'd made of *Casabl*anca, but straight afterwards, the plantigrade emitted a moan, turned toward the mountain, and walked away at an even pace.

I then swore to myself that if I ever met Rick Blaine in heaven, I'd remind him to never let go and not to underestimate bluffing as a strategy. I also thought of dear Haemon, who should have screamed at his father rather than self-mutilate in front of him while his betrothed was being walled up.

All the tension accumulated in my body disappeared, and I adjusted the pig on my shoulder before carrying on along my path.

Was it my shout or the lightning that had scared the bear, or both? It didn't matter, after all. If fate had any more traps for me, then it could go ahead and set them. I felt indestructible.

I thought about Emma and what I was going to say to her.

Nothing. Words would be for later. I was going to take her in my arms, hold her tight, and kiss her for as long as possible, then start again until she told me I was overdoing it.

She, too, had been betrayed, and when she had met me, despite my limitations as a dancer and all my reservations, she must have somehow sensed that we had something in common. Actually, that had also happened to me. Is it seriously realistic that a guy as cautious as I tried to be could go chasing after a stranger at Menton station just because of a simple slap and a few deleted lines? If I'd offered to drive her, which was tantamount to following her, it was definitely because I had felt the bond between us, despite appearances to the contrary.

We belonged to the same family, she and I. That of children who had been betrayed, humiliated, and disappointed. I now understood so well how she must have felt. To suddenly see that father, who'd taught her to dive, brought back treasures with her, and then shared them innocently on the beach, turn into a bad cop. How could he have changed to that point? Because of a problem at work? His libido? A lithium deficiency? Grown-ups always had an excuse for becoming bastards, but we, the children, were fed up with excuses, and Emma especially. She had chosen insubordination. She'd found a door in a hazelnut tree that led to another world, where kings had wooden swords, where bicycle pyramids were erected and you danced barefoot at any time of day. I love you so much, Emma. It's true that you could be my daughter, but I'm your child, too. And I think you worked that out. Before I did.

Still, there was something wonderful about life, a magical side in the midst of these lost battles and these millions of living dead who catch planes and trains with or without their caps, and not just the fact that a Florida resident disguised as a coconut tree could reconcile a pig killer with his past, but that Emma and I should have recognized each other beyond

230 - ALAIN GILLOT

our differences and perhaps even been reassured by them. This way, we would each have our own areas of expertise, and neither would take the upper hand over the other. This was not a domination exercise but a journey where one would take the wheel when the other one slept.

I stepped over a hedge, and the thorns scratched my ankles, but I paid no attention. I didn't feel anything anymore, I just had my eyes on the barn, which was getting nearer and nearer. And, as the curtain of rain got less thick, I noticed that the ground ahead was lighter. Raphaël had managed to fix the projector, and its light also spread outside.

In a second, I saw parade before me the faces of all those I'd met during this detour that wasn't one. Talking of casting, Leonardo could go change right out of his costume, with his tin-pot remake! The brother, the mother as guest stars, the nurse at the Toulouse University hospital, that wretched Zoll who only directed himself, Victor, Raphaël, Béatrice, Émilie, Boris, the Iranian hotel owner and his family. The airport guard and the former special services man, then the mayor, Uztai, his grandmother, the great Sarah, Imanol, as well as the dog, and the improbable Agustin, my savior forever! There was no reason not to add the others, Cécile and Belmer, Tosik and Carole; even the bespoke bathing suit specialist could be listed in the credits. I didn't know him, but I was certain that he, too, had his baggage, we all do. The checkroom was full. It was impossible to rummage through it all. Sometimes, it's better to blow it up and move on.

I realized I was losing my skirt. Oh, no. Not now. Fate wanted to poke fun at me to the very end. I then remembered that I'd kept at my belt—no doubt as a remnant of the well-organized man I had been—a pouch with my papers and money, where I'd put the present from the twins, the button and the safety pin. It was still there, and I was able to restore my self-respect by tightening the fabric with the safety pin, provisionally, of course, but seemingly reliably. Everything came in useful on a journey, apparently. The button would be for later.

I saw again the dear faces of the twins, playing in the dust of the waste ground, so free, so happy. Two queens who had no intention of letting Creon take power.

What was grown-ups' problem with children? Were they scared of them? Didn't they see the opportunity they gave to remind them to live? All these battered, humiliated, forgotten children, what had they done to the world to deserve this? Except come out of their mothers' bellies. Did people want to wall them up alive, too? Because they were too noisy? Because children's noise was such a big deal, after all, the din of their wishes, that one was tempted to silence them. But that time was over. At least for me. I would not cut any more screen-plays, and I would no longer content myself with hitting the ball, I was leaving the tennis court once and for all, I was going to write my own story and that of my family, my real one, the one that sings in the squares and can make poems even out of the garbage thrown at them.

I walked along the stream to the exact spot where Victor had talked to me about my fear, when I was unable to tell him where it came from. I had covered so much ground since then. I walked a little farther, then looked up and saw Emma. She was standing outside the barn, the light behind her, and her outline against the light said everything about her. Her won-derful pride, which I was getting to know, her grace, which turned her rebellion into honey. How did she know I was com-ing? Perhaps my shout had really carried all the way here. So many apparently unlikely things had happened over the past few days.

I walked up the mound and stood before her, neither above nor below, at the level of her eyes. Those insubordinate eyes of hers.

"You have a pig on your shoulder," she said. "It must be a bit heavy."

"No, it's alright," I said, putting it down.

"Is it the rain, or are you crying?"

"Excuse me?"

"You look like you're crying."

I quickly rubbed my fist over my eyes.

"It's true. I'm crying."

"I thought you never did."

"I've changed a lot, recently."

"You keep strange company."

"I think so, too."

"Do you think it might end badly?"

"Not necessarily."

She was very close. What would we start with? It was good to wait but not too long. Then Raphaël came out of the barn. Oh, no, I thought, not him. Not now.

"O seekers of illusions! O exhausted travelers! Harken to the humble storyteller who brings misery and marvel! Let it be said with moderation that happiness is but a dream!"

I have to be honest, at that moment, I wasn't really listening to the words, their music was more than enough for me. I vaguely heard Boris tell Raphaël to shut up and that Creon wanted to see the pig. But that was no longer my concern. I'd done my bit. I was kissing Emma hard, I was holding her hand, and that was all.